THE DEADLY WEDDING

Abigail Summers Cozy Mysteries
Book 5

ANN PARKER

Copyright © 2025 Ann Parker

Layout design and Copyright © 2025 by Next Chapter

Published 2025 by Next Chapter

Cover design by Lordan June Pinote

This book is a work of fiction. Names, characters, places, and incidents are the product of the author's imagination or are used fictitiously. Any resemblance to actual events, locales, or persons, living or dead, is purely coincidental.

All rights reserved. No part of this book may be reproduced or transmitted in any form or by any means, electronic or mechanical, including photocopying, recording, or by any information storage and retrieval system, without the author's permission.

More books by Ann Parker

The Deadly Detective Agency

The Deadly Pub Quiz

The Deadly Regatta

The Deadly Fun Run

*Dedicated to all my friends and family
who read my books, and especially those I don't know,
who take a chance and read one.
Thank you very much x*

Wedding Invitation

Colonel Henry & Harriet Newberry
request the presence of
Tom & Hayley Bennett

at the wedding of their daughter,
Amelia, to Daniel Templeton

on
March 10th at 3 pm at
St Barnabas Church, Micklebrook.
Reception to follow at Micklebrook Priory.

RSVP ASAP

Chapter 1

"Who the hell are Amelia and Daniel?" asked Tom after he saw the invitation while getting ready for work at Gorebridge Police Station.

"I have no idea. I assumed they were friends of yours," answered Hayley. "It just came."

"I knew a Danny from police training, but not well enough to be invited to a posh do at Micklebrook Priory."

"Same here. I seem to remember an Amelia from school, but we weren't that close. How strange. And it's less than a month away, which makes me think we're a bit of an afterthought. I don't remember getting a save-the-date card."

"I suppose we could go and then eat and run."

"I could do the eating part," Hayley said while rubbing her belly. "I'll be huge by then." The psychic medium had not seen that coming. She was now pregnant and would be six months when the wedding took place.

"Good, you can eat for two."

"And what would I wear? I suppose I could go to the tent shop."

Tom put his coat on, moved her long black hair to one side

and kissed her cheek. "You'll be the most beautiful one there. But we might not go yet. I'll ask at work in case anyone else got one. Perhaps it's one of the detectives or something. Although they wouldn't ask a lowly constable."

"I'll ring round as well. Can you imagine how embarrassing it would be if we got an invitation by mistake and it's meant for another Tom and Hayley?"

"Well, I'll be off. Bye, Luna. Behave yourself."

Luna, who meowed in answer, was getting quite big now. He had first come into their lives after they found a near-dead kitten whose mother had died. He was like their baby, and they worried what he would think of this new life suddenly arriving in the coming months.

"Stay safe, hun. And ring me if anything exciting happens," Hayley reminded him.

"You mean if there's anything that the Deadly Detective Agency can look into?"

"No, I'm just being my normal caring self, hun."

"Hmm. Well, take it easy, and I'll see you tonight."

Hayley was hoping there would be a case for them soon. Apart from the odd missing will and lost pets, the last one they had was months ago. A woman and her husband had been shot in the back after he made a deal with some particularly nasty people in Gorebridge. Even then, they hadn't done much, as the bullets had proved who had shot the Newsomes rather than their sleuthing. Although it was thanks to them that the police had known they were dead, as the ghost of Carol Newsome was found wandering about by Abigail. Even their nemesis, Tom's boss, Detective Chief Inspector Johnson, had managed to arrest the gang and its boss, Martin Reagan. He usually needed their help but didn't realise it.

"I'm just going to chill out with Luna, and I might have another go at knitting. Actually, thinking about it, he's always getting hold of the wool. Maybe that's why my shawl looks like bubble wrap."

"Yes, it's the cat's fault," laughed Tom as he walked out the door.

So as soon as Tom had left, Abigail Summers, dressmaker in life, sleuth in death, walked into Hayley's kitchen—through the wall. Not that Tom could have seen her; the only one that could do that was Hayley Bennett, or Hayley Moon when she was working as a psychic medium. Abigail had been walking into her house for the past year, ever since she was killed at the age of thirty-nine and her friend, Hayley, along with a group of fellow ghosts, had helped her catch the murderer. After that, they started the agency and had many clients—some alive, some dead.

"Anybody would think you were waiting for Tom to leave," said Hayley.

"As if. Of course not," lied Abigail. It could get really boring being dead. She had spent all night with the other spirits at the Becklesfield Public Library at the foot of the Chiltern Hills, and she, too, could do with a new case. "How is our little Benjie this morning?"

"Kicking like he's going to be a footballer. Either that or he's doing somersaults. I hope he's not this active when he's born."

"I think they sleep all the time to start with. Not that I know about these things. Anything happening in the world of the living? Ooh, are we off to a wedding?" asked Abigail.

"I'm not even sure we're going yet, hun. We have no idea who the bride and groom are."

"Amelia Newberry and Daniel Templeton. I haven't heard of them. But I did know a Harriet Newberry who was married to a colonel. I shortened all her curtains for her when she moved house. Very posh. To be honest, I can't imagine you moving in her circles, Hayl—no offence."

"Charming. But you're right. I don't think either of us knows them."

"I wonder why you got an invite then. Could it be something to do with you being a psychic? Or they saw your advert for the Deadly Detective Agency?"

"I have no idea, so I'm not a very good one. Tom's going to check at work." Hayley suddenly went quiet and gave a faraway look. "But I have a funny idea I'm about to find out."

"Awesome. Have you had a paranormal premonition?"

Hayley laughed. "No, I can see a woman getting out of her car through the window."

Both Hayley and Abigail heard a car door slam outside in Church Lane, followed by footsteps leading up to the front door.

Chapter 2

"Hayley, it's lovely to see you again. Did you get my wedding invitation?"

"Amelia? I did. But I couldn't place you till now, so forgive me if I seem surprised. Come in. We were at school together, weren't we?"

"Yes. You left, and I carried on into the sixth form and went to university to study art. I own a gallery now."

"You can see why I'm so shocked that you invited me to your wedding then. Especially as it seems like a very grand affair."

"Well, Mummy and Daddy are paying, so why not? Danny and I are thinking of eloping now. There's so much hard work that goes into organising a wedding, and we've got a wedding planner. She's very good—May Palmer of May's Days. But congratulations to you as well. I had no idea you were expecting. Quite soon, by the looks of it. I hope you don't have it on the day of the wedding. A bride doesn't like to be overshadowed, you know."

"I'll still be weeks away by then. But why have you invited us, hun? To be honest, I can't remember us being besties or anything. We were in the same class, but that's about it."

"Hmm, this is going to sound rather weird, actually, Hayley."

"You'd be surprised how often I hear that," said Hayley, looking at Abigail, who was sitting, unseen, right next to Amelia.

"I've been following your career, and Mum went to a couple of your talks for the Women's Institute. Your professional name is Hayley Moon, isn't it? So I asked around and got your married name and address. The thing is, do you remember at school you would do that thing where you'd tell people their fortunes or would say what was going to happen?"

"I do. Everyone thought I was a bit strange, so I used it to my advantage. It made me slightly more popular. It was just a bit of fun, though. So what's this about?"

"It was after school one day at Donna's house. Do you remember her? You told her that she would break her arm skiing when she went on holiday."

"Yes, but she was accident-prone, so it would have been a good bet."

"And you told Vicky that she would score eight goals in netball, and the next day she did. You even predicted that Miss Gilmour, the English teacher, would get the sack. And loads of other times you were right. But also that day, you told me something that I hadn't remembered till yesterday."

"I have no idea what I said, hun."

"I was actually talking to May Palmer, the wedding planner, and she reminded me exactly what you said. We were talking about the day itself, and she thought that my wedding would be the talk of the county."

"That's good, isn't it?"

"Not necessarily. You told me, and I quote, 'You will meet someone with the initials DT.'"

"Oh wow, I am good," smiled Hayley.

"But that's not it. You said the same as her, that 'my wedding would be the talk of the county—for all the wrong reasons. So be careful'. Of course, we all laughed and said how spooky or funny or something. But now I'm not laughing. I'm rather scared."

Abigail said, "Oh dear, you're in trouble, Hayley."

Hayley ignored her and felt awful. "I really have no memory of that, Amelia. That was so long ago, and the future is never the same. Different things happen to change the course of things. I've been wrong many times."

"No, you haven't," butted in Abigail.

Hayley carried on, "I'm sure you haven't got anything to worry about, hun. In those days, I just said the first thing that came into my head. Most of the time, it was rubbish. If you say enough things, you're bound to be right sometimes. Take Miss Gilmour, for instance—she was a bit too friendly with some of the sixth formers."

"But you got the initials right, so why not the rest?"

"If it helps, I'm not getting a feeling of any great disaster that's going to happen. I'll try to think about it when I have more time, just to make sure. My mind hasn't been quite so clear since I've been pregnant."

"Please try, Hayley. That's why I invited you. If anything happens on the day, you'll be there to warn me."

"If it's in the stars, I won't be able to stop it."

"You might if it's something like my strapless dress is about to fall down or someone has put poison in the cake."

That made Abigail sit forward. She loved a good poisoning. "You better go, Hayl. Just in case."

"Oh goodness, don't even think of that. But who is making your cake?" joked Hayley.

"Saloni Kaye. She runs A Slice of Nice in Little Beckles from home. She was recommended by May. I went there with my mother the other day. She's the bridezilla, not me. We had to go right through the details again. We're having four tiers, and Mum wanted to taste one of the layers. We're having one chocolate, one vanilla, and one lemon, but she wanted to try a red velvet for the top layer. Probably why I'm thinking it might be poisoning in the cake is because a man burst in when we were there and got very abusive."

"With you?"

"No, with Saloni. He accused her of pinching one of his customers. I tell you, weddings are a very cutthroat business, Hayley. Too many people trying to sell you their services and not enough weddings."

"That is true. Tom and I used to go to a lot of weddings, and yours is the first invitation we've had for ages. And even that's not for the pleasure of our scintillating company."

"Of course it is. I'd love you and Tom to come. Perhaps we could go out for a foursome before then. To get to know each other. You'll know a few people there. Donna is actually my maid of honour. Mind you, that upset my sister, Charlotte; she thought it would be her. But we don't get on, so she's just a normal bridesmaid. The other two are Danny's stepsisters. Please come, Hayley. We've got a disco and dancing in the evening. And you needn't get us a present."

"I don't know about the dancing, but you had me at four-tiered cake," said Hayley, patting her stomach. "And of course we'll get you a present."

"Well, there's a list online if you insist, but just get something small. I'm so pleased you're coming. I feel better with you as a part of it. Like I'll get a warning."

"I really don't think that you've got anything to worry about." But Hayley had a sudden feeling of dread, and her eyes went to the ghost sitting by Amelia.

"Oh my God, Hayley. You've seen something. You look like you've seen a ghost."

"I often do, but it's not that. I have a funny feeling that something has literally just happened, but it's nothing to do with you."

The Deadly Wedding

They all jumped when Hayley's phone started to ring, and she excused herself, going into the kitchen. She returned after a minute with a worried look on her face.

"That was Tom; he's a police constable if you didn't know. You know when you said weddings were a cutthroat business? You weren't wrong. What was the name of your cakemaker?"

"Saloni Kaye from A Slice of Nice. Why?"

"She's just been found with her throat cut!"

Amelia's hand went to her neck. "You're kidding. What about my cake? Sorry, that's a bit selfish. Poor lady. Does he know who did it?"

"No, not yet. They haven't long had the call-out. Tell me about her."

"She's about forty or fiftyish. Married, and I think her children have left home or gone to uni, maybe. I have no idea what the husband does. Must be something that pays well, as they have a really nice house. Her business is in an extension on the side."

"Is she busy?"

"Very. She doesn't just do celebration cakes—she makes cupcakes and biscuits for the local bakers."

"And you were told about her by May Palmer, the wedding planner? What about the other baker that came in the other day?"

"Was it him, do you think? Oh God, and we're witnesses. He might be after us now."

"All the more reason to tell me what you know about him. Who was it?"

"Saloni apologised after he left, and I can't remember his name, but he owned Cakealicious. He was swearing and said she'd lost him five hundred pounds. And she'd better not cross him again or else she'd be bleep bleep sorry. She told us that he was due to make a cake for a wedding at the end of February, but they cancelled and told him they wanted her to make it. But she said it was nothing to do with her. Saloni was actually quite scared, and I don't blame her. He was a big bloke, and I wouldn't want him as an enemy."

"I'll tell Tom when I speak to him next, and he can pass it on. But they'll probably want you to give a statement. They'll need to talk to him and find out where he was when she was killed. And your mum went with you, not Danny?"

"Yes. He was working, and to be honest, I think he gets sick and tired of all the little things we have to do. I get the feeling that he'll be glad when it's all over. And I feel the same now."

"It's understandable. We had a small wedding, and that took a lot of time and worry. It's a lot to do for one day. To say nothing of all the money it takes," added Hayley.

"Mum paid for most of it. Apart from my dress. I've just had the final fitting. I bought it from Belle Bridal, and I didn't want her to have any say in that. I dread to think what she would have me in. I wonder if this is the thing that will make my wedding talked about—my cakemaker being murdered."

"Maybe if she was killed on that day."

"I know you're pregnant and everything, but do you think you could look into the murder for me? You know, ask Tom if there's any connection to my wedding."

"I suppose I could, Amelia. But don't get too excited that I can do anything. I do know a few people who could help. No, you don't know them. They run a detective agency. There's Abigail and her friends Terry, Betty, Lillian, and Suzie. We'll see what we can do, I promise. So tell me where Saloni lived."

"It's Baytree Lodge at the end of the high street in Little Beckles."

Hayley looked at Abigail, just in time to see her disappear through the wall to make her way to the library. The Deadly Detective Agency had a new case at last.

Chapter 3

DETECTIVE CHIEF INSPECTOR TONY JOHNSON LIKED the village of Little Beckles straight away—mainly because it had three pubs in its short high street. Very handy if he wrapped up this murder quickly. And his sergeant, Dave Mills, was driving.

They went past the last pub, the Royal Stag, and stopped outside a large Tudor house called Baytree Lodge. The yellow tape was blowing in the wind, keeping out a few of the villagers who had bothered to find out what was going on. He rolled his eyes when he saw PC Tom Bennett standing on the other side of it. He'd better not interfere with his case again. He had a habit of solving his murders before he did. He didn't know for sure, but some said it was with the help of his hippy wife. Sergeant Mills knew this was true and had no problem getting to the top on young Tom's coattails.

Tom was rubbing his hands together to keep warm and held the tape up for his bosses to enter.

"What have we got, Bennett?"

"The doctor and forensics are in there at the moment, sir. Photographs have been taken. All I know for sure is that her name is Saloni Kaye. I had a quick look around, and there's no sign that it's a robbery. Nothing appears to have been taken. She's a baker who specialises in cakes. She was found by the couple over there who had come for their eleven o'clock appointment about their wedding cake. It wasn't a pretty sight; she'd had her throat cut, and there was a lot of blood."

"Any weapon at the scene?" asked his friend and sergeant, Dave Mills.

"Right next to the body. A fancy silver cake knife. The couple said they had seen it there. It was part of a display that you could rent for the day, with a matching cake stand."

Johnson snapped, "I'll bear it in mind if I ever get the urge for the third time. Show me the body, lad."

Tom led them round the side of the house and into a new brick building that was joined on. There was a desk where the owner sat and two chairs opposite for her clients. The display cabinet was to the side, and in the centre was the silver cake stand that Tom had mentioned.

"The body is through here, sir, where she did the actual baking. It's not really a bakery so much as a cakery. She just did cakes and cupcake-type things."

"Morning, doc. Not a pretty sight," said Johnson to the well-built doctor.

"Morning, Tony. No, very violent. She was on her stomach with her face to one side. I've rolled her over to do a quick examination." Saloni Kaye looked like she had been cooking, as she was wearing a bright white tabard, and there were bowls and ingredients on the work surface.

"What do you know so far?" Johnson asked the doctor.

"Obviously, her throat has been cut. From a quick look at the depth of the cut, she was killed from behind by a right-handed assailant."

"Man or woman?"

"That's for you to decide."

He held up a large knife in an evidence bag. "A serrated edge, so it would have taken a lot of force. And she would have bled out in less than a minute. Nasty way to go. No rigor yet. Maybe an hour or so ago. Don't hold me to it, but I'd say between nine and ten."

"Any prints on the knife?"

"I'm told not, I'm afraid."

"Thanks, doc. Bennett, what do we know about the husband? Hopefully, it's him. It usually is."

"Not much. I spoke to one of the neighbours out there, and he said his name is Darren, and he leaves for work every day at about eight. Both in their forties. It was just the two of them after the kids left home. We haven't been able to locate him yet. Would you like me to search the rest of the house and find his details and where he'd be?"

"Leave that to us two. You stand outside this door and stop anyone coming in. Mills, go and talk to that couple that found the body. Get their details, and they can go. She looks young, but he's old enough to know better."

"Maybe it's his second marriage, sir."

"Precisely, that's my point. What an idiot. Why would they want to spend all that money on the worst day of their lives? Matrimony? Matrimoany, I call it."

Mills had to smile at his boss sometimes. He walked back outside to where a couple were facing each other and holding hands. She looked shocked but also rather excited. He heard the words 'post it later', and then she stopped talking as he was seen approaching. She was definitely a good twenty years younger than her boyfriend.

"I'm Sergeant Mills," he said as he took out his notebook. "Could I have your names, please?"

The lady wiped away an imaginary tear. "Colleen Wilson and William Murphy."

"How are you feeling? I hear it was you who found the

body."

"It was the worst thing that has ever happened to me. I'll never get over it."

"I'm sure, miss. Was this your first appointment with the deceased?"

The man spoke for the first time. "No, it's our second visit. We came last week to get a few ideas and prices, and we came back to tell her that we had decided to use her after all. We were going to go with this other bloke, but we heard a lot of bad things about him. So we came to put down a deposit and try some samples."

"Now, did you see anyone coming out or leaving the house? Or in the vicinity, before or after?"

"No one at all, did we, love? Colleen and I were just talking about that."

"Any cars?"

"Hmm, there was a white van going along. But there always are these days."

"Any writing on the side?"

"If there was, I can't remember it," admitted William. "There was a woman and a child walking down the opposite side of the high street as I parked. But I don't think I could describe them. I've never been that good at faces."

Colleen bit her lip and said, "I did hear something though, Sergeant Mills. Does that help?"

"Everything helps, miss."

"It was a dog yelping and barking. Quite a big dog, I would say. It wasn't like a little squeak-type thing. Did Saloni have a dog, Will? It seemed to come from that way. It was just after I got out of the car. I can't remember a dog last time we came, but it definitely came from behind her house. But I think there might be a park there somewhere."

"I'll check, thank you. Right, so you knocked and waited for her to let you in, did you?"

The Deadly Wedding

They looked at each other. "No, we just went in this time because the door was slightly open," said Colleen. "We shouted hello, then we looked in the other room. She had shown us around when we came before, so we weren't worried about going in there. And there she was. Of course, I screamed, and Will had a closer look to see if she was still alive. Then we ran for our lives and called you."

"For all we knew, the murderer could have still been there."

"You did the right thing, sir. And the knife was next to her?"

"By her head. We didn't touch anything, I can assure you. As I told the other policeman, she had shown us the knife last time we came. She was very proud of it. Apparently, it's an expensive antique—early Victorian. She bought that and the matching stand from an auction at an old manor house in Bedfordshire. She loved it. Very ironic. I suppose someone grabbed it in a fit of temper."

"More than likely. How did you hear about her?"

"From our wedding planner—May," said Colleen proudly. "It's my first wedding, and Will said I can spend as much as I want." Will didn't look quite so happy about that fact.

"Could I have her full name, please?"

"May Palmer, who runs May's Days. She charges a fortune, but it's worth it, isn't it, Will?" Again, Will didn't look like he agreed.

"When you can, could you come to Gorebridge Police Station and give a formal statement? And please try and think of anything else that comes to mind. Could I have your address first, please?"

"Addresses," said Colleen smugly. "We're not married yet, so separate beds," she laughed. Again, Will was not pleased.

"Oh, did you arrive together?"

"Er, no. I work night shifts sometimes, so I drove here straight from work, and Colleen got here a few minutes after me."

"That's right. I wondered where he was to start with, but he was waiting by the door."

No alibi for him then, thought Dave.

On the way back inside, he told Tom to get another uniformed officer to talk to all the neighbours. "Start with asking them if they saw Mr Kaye leave and anything that happened until the police arrived. Oh, and ask if the Kayes had a dog. The lady heard a dog yelping when she got here. Could be nothing, but you never know."

He went back to find his boss talking to the doctor and telling the police photographer to take some photos of the display cabinet. All prints had been wiped off there as well.

"You can take the body now, doc. I've seen enough. It'll put me off my pint else. We'll stop for a quick one in *The* Royal Stag when we've finished here, Mills. As part of our enquiries with the locals, of course."

"Of course, sir. Shall we do a quick search of the house first? Find out the next of kin? There's no mobile phone here, so it might be in the main house. I'm presuming it's through that door there. And we've got to check if there's a dog. Miss Wilson thought she heard one as she arrived."

"Well, let's not hang about, Sergeant. I'm getting rather thirsty."

It was at that point that Abigail spoke for the first time. They had got there just before Johnson had arrived and were listening to all that was said. The other spirits that rushed over to Little Beckles as soon as they heard the news were Lillian Yin, a nurse in life and still in her navy uniform, and Suzie, a beautiful black girl she looked after in the afterlife, who was very good in any situation as she was the only one who could move things. Good for finding clues and also good for haunting, as they had found out. Suzie had been killed by a drunk driver on her way to a friend's birthday party when she was nine years old.

"I thought they'd never go," said Abigail. "Have a look at the body, Lillian. Suzie, you look the other way—it's not for someone your age. Do you agree with the time of death?"

"The blood has only just started to coagulate, and there's no rigor mortis, so I reckon between nine and ten. Probably nearer nine."

"The dog is a bit of a funny thing," said Abigail thoughtfully. "The curious incident of the dog that yelped in the nighttime, you could say."

Lillian and Suzie looked puzzled. "I thought it yelped when they got here."

"I didn't mean it literally. Well, maybe literary. Honestly, sometimes I'm wasted on you lot," to which the other two just rolled their eyes and shrugged.

"All I mean is, if the dog was hurt by the murderer at that point, what was he still doing here? Maybe he was looking for something or doing something. Come on, let's keep up with Johnson and Mills. We'll follow them around and see what they see."

The two policemen had got as far as the family kitchen, which was tidy as well as modern. "No sign of a dog bowl. Perhaps it was just a dog outside, sir."

"I don't think that's important, Mills. There's always a dog somewhere. Hmm, the back door is unlocked. The murderer could have got in or out this way. It's a lot less overlooked than the front. Nice big garden. Pretty much surrounded by trees, and over there is the park, isn't it?"

"Would make sense they used this way. But we can't rule out that the murderer came in the front to see her, grabbed the knife after an argument, saw red and killed her in a temper. I'll get the boys to check round the back as well as the neighbours," Mills told him.

Abigail frowned. "I disagree with what happened. I don't think it was spontaneous at all. The knife was in a cabinet in the other room. I don't know if you noticed, but there was a block of knives on the worktop next to where she was found. Why not just grab one of those? I feel this was a statement killing. That knife meant something. Once we get a few more clues, we might know why."

Johnson had found the dining room, where there was a writing desk. "Have a look through that, Sergeant."

On top was Saloni's phone. "No password needed; that's good. Here we are. I've got the husband's number. Darren, wasn't it? I'd rather go and see him, though. Here's the name of his firm, Anexis. It's not that far. Do you mind if I leave now, sir?" asked Mills.

"No, son. You do that. I'm going to carry on my enquiries in the Royal Stag. I'll get someone to drive me back to Gorebridge, and then they can carry on with the search. Right, I'll be off. It's a hard job, but someone's got to do it," Johnson said as he thought of his cold pint of beer.

"If you'd rather, you could do the notification, and I'll go and ask around in the pub?"

"No, Sergeant, you are a lot more diplomatic than me. Tell him we'll need him to formally identify the body as soon as he can. I'll see you later."

Lillian said, "Ain't that the truth. He'd probably tell him his wife is dead and then, in the next breath, say he was going to arrest him."

"What are we going to do now?" asked Suzie excitedly.

"We'll have to wait and see what Tom finds out, so I think we should go back to Hayley's and tell her what we know. We've got one dead woman, a very expensive murder weapon, a dog who could be a witness and one, two, three suspects. What a good day to be a sleuth!"

The Deadly Wedding

Abigail, Lillian and Suzie stopped off at the Becklesfield Public Library to pick up the other two deceased members of The Deadly Detective Agency. The eldest was Betty, who was eighty-two when she died a few years ago. She had been married to John for sixty years and had died a week after him, so this was her me-time. Keeping her company was Terry Styles, who had died in the 1980s. He was a handsome but grumpy, middle-aged man. Although he was ten years older than the pretty blonde Abigail, they got on very well, and love had been mentioned on more than one occasion. She could drive him up the wall, but her blue eyes and beguiling smile helped.

Terry, Betty and the others had quite a boring death just sitting around in the Becklesfield Library—until Abigail Summers had been murdered and insisted they help to find out who killed her. Something they could quite understand to start with, as she was bossy and took charge. But in the end, they grew to enjoy her company and loved that she had got them to form The Deadly Detective Agency. Now there was another case for them to unravel.

They all made their way to Hayley's house in Church Lane, the one with the dreamcatcher and the wind chimes in the porch. Lillian, Suzie and Abigail told the others what had happened at the scene, and they soon all knew what was going on. They agreed that William Murphy was the first person who should be checked.

"I'll tell Tom he needs to find out what time he left work this morning after his night shift. He was on the scene before or just after she was attacked. So why didn't he say that he had heard a dog?" said Hayley.

"Exactly. Maybe because he was inside," added Abigail. "And we have the husband, Darren, and the cakemaker who burst in when Amelia was there."

Lillian spoke, "That reminds me, William's girlfriend,

Colleen, said that they were going to have someone else but changed their minds when they heard bad things about him."

"I checked into him on my phone after you'd gone," said Hayley. "His name is Chris Jenkins, and he started Cakealicious about three years ago. He wasn't on May's website, and there are quite a few recommendations, like Saloni, but not him."

"So someone has been giving him a bad name," said Betty.

"So we've got a plan of action to start with," said Abigail. "Someone needs to go and see May Palmer and Mr Cakealicious. Hayley, what about your baby shower?"

"I'm not having one, as you well know."

"But he doesn't know that, does he? You should go and talk to him about it."

"Well, I will be needing a christening cake."

"You can kill two stones with one bush," said Betty, who had a habit of getting her sayings wrong or back to front. But it was part of her charm.

"It's a bit early for that. But you could be thinking of a baby shower and just order his smallest cake," said Lillian.

"Well, I do like cake. Maybe a little one. I wouldn't want to be rude, and it will be less suspicious if I actually order one. Tom will go mad if I put myself in danger again."

"Suzie can go with you for protection." Suzie had saved Hayley's life on more than one occasion, with a shove or by grabbing a potential murder weapon. "Or you could do it over the phone," added Terry.

"No, I like a face-to-face meeting. Get a feel of him. Not literally, of course."

"Well, don't do or say anything to make him wary."

"Me? Of course not. And I've got a good cover story. He can see that I'm pregnant. So what are you lot going to do?"

"Obviously, you can't go and see the wedding planner, Hayley, but Terry, it's about time you and I tied the knot," suggested Abigail.

"Well, I have thought about one around your neck sometimes," he said with a grin.

"Haha. That's close enough. We could go and have a nose around and hopefully be there while someone else has an appointment. She could say something that helps."

"Good idea, Mrs Styles. We'll go tomorrow."

"I'm still Miss Summers till you make an honest woman of me."

"Oh dear, dear," said Betty. "What's that saying about your letters and bad luck?"

"What sort of letters, hun?"

"Not written ones. The S in their surnames. I'll get it in a minute." The others all started to look busy, and Hayley looked at her watch. It never took a minute.

"Now, it was something like you better change your letter and your name. No, that's wrong. Change your name for the better and not a letter. I'm nearly there. Change a letter, er, I've got it. Change your name and not the letter, change for worse and not for better!"

But everybody had gone. The first time she had got it right, and everyone had gone. Typical, Betty thought.

Chapter 4

SERGEANT MILLS FOUND A SPACE IN THE CAR PARK AT Saloni's husband's firm. He switched off the engine and made no effort to get out of the car. He enjoyed his job. He found all aspects of a murder enquiry exciting, but not this. He had to tell this poor man that his wife had been murdered in one of the most awful ways, and his whole life would never be the same again. He never knew whether to say it quickly or lead up to it, so it wasn't so much of a shock. But it was always a shock. He blew out his cheeks and made for the entrance of Anexis.

The pretty receptionist smiled and asked him if he had an appointment. He showed her his badge, and she rang through, then pointed the way to Darren Kaye's office. As they usually did, Darren made a joke and invited him to sit down.

"I'm really sorry to tell you that I have some awful news about your wife. Her name is Saloni?"

"Yes, Saloni. What's happened? Has there been an accident?"

"I'm afraid she's dead, sir." He paused while Kaye went back in his seat and put both hands over his mouth. "She was murdered, Mr Kaye. I really am so sorry." Dave knew the recommended phrase was 'I'm sorry for your loss'. But everyone said

The Deadly Wedding

that, and now it didn't seem sincere. It was almost like they had just learned the words.

"Murdered? At our house? That doesn't happen in our village. Was it a burglary or something? She wasn't assaulted in that way, was she?"

"No, sir, nothing like that. And she died very quickly. They will do an autopsy and find out exactly how." It was a bit of a white lie to save him from more heartache. How could he say his wife had had her throat cut by her own knife? He didn't want to think about it, let alone say it.

"But why then? Have you any idea who would do it?"

"It's early in the investigation, but we have a big team working on it. They're currently checking the village for any witnesses. But can you think of anyone who would want to harm Saloni?"

"No, of course not. She was a great mum and made cakes for a living. She gave to charities and went to keep fit in the village. That's about all."

"When was the last time you saw her?"

"This morning. We had tea and toast together at about half past seven, and then I left for work. I kissed her goodbye like I always do and ..." Darren had to stop talking but stopped himself from sobbing. "Now you say she's gone, just like that."

"Did you see anyone in the road or see anything unusual?"

"Not that I can think of. But I'll think it over later. I can't at the moment. I have to ring my children. And Saloni's mum. God knows what I'll say to her."

"We'll need details of your children's names and numbers when you're up to it. They might know something."

"Of course. They don't live with us anymore, but we're a close family. The girls are married, and our son is at university in Hatfield."

"No rush, sir. We will need you to formally identify your wife and write a statement. Probably tomorrow if you can. But please try and think if your wife mentioned anything that could help us."

"I will. Actually, she did say that someone had burst into an appointment she had and accused her of taking his clients off him. I think he was from Delicious Cakes or something. She tried to say she didn't know what he was talking about, but he was mad as hell, she said. Saloni didn't need to do that. She had plenty of work. Too much, actually. She was thinking of cutting out weddings altogether. She found them very stressful. Do you think it could be him? If he did, you'd better tell him to watch his back." Darren's nostrils flared in anger, and his lips tightened. He preferred the feeling of anger to sadness.

"Has she always made cakes, sir?"

"She started when our children had their birthday parties. Over the years, she made pirate ships, castles, and mermaids, and other parents asked her to make one for them. At first, she did it as a favour, but she was so busy she started to charge in the end. Then, when the kids grew older, she took a job in Gorebridge in a bespoke cake firm. Must have been about ten years ago. They were sorry when she left. A lot of clients asked for her by name. And then a few years back, she started her own business, and we had the extension built for her. I think it was the happiest day of her life when she got that first order. And the customers were always happy and often sent her a photo of the cutting of the cake."

"We might need a list of all her clients."

"She wrote everything down in a book. Old school. Not on a computer. It will be in her office somewhere. Probably on her desk."

"Did they collect the cake from you? Might you have seen some of them?"

"Yes, they did, except for the wedding cakes. Saloni delivered them to the venues on the day. Or sometimes the day before. But if it had tiers, she would want to put it together."

"Tell me about the silver cake knife and stand."

"She loved them and used to rent them out for quite a lot of money. She got them at an estate sale at a country house. Why? Why are they important?"

"I can't tell you any more at the moment, sir."

"Well, if that's all, I'd like to get on, Sergeant."

Mills stood up, and Darren Kaye walked him to the door.

"I don't like to ask, Mr Kaye, but what time did you arrive this morning?"

"I'm always here by eight-thirty. My receptionist can confirm that. I know the quicker you can rule me out, the quicker you can catch the one that did it."

"Thank you, sir. Not everyone is so understanding. What exactly do you do here at Anexis?"

"We're an events company. We arrange conferences and bespoke dinners for clients in engineering and technology, to make a safe and sustainable future for the next generation. Not that I care about that anymore."

There must be a lot of money in it, thought Mills as he went back to his car and looked up at the new building. He got back in the car, wishing he could join Johnson in the pub. He deserved a stiff drink himself. But he'd go back to the crime scene until he could go home to his wife and young daughter. He didn't often get home before the little one was in bed, but today he needed to see his family. Mills knew better than most that life wasn't set. Anything could happen to your world in one swipe of a blade.

Chapter 5

HAYLEY RANG CHRIS OF CAKEALICIOUS AND MADE AN appointment for the following morning. He wanted to go to her house, but she didn't want him to know where she lived; he could be a murderer, after all. So they met at the Willow Tea Room in Gorebridge. Hayley noticed a small white van with a cake logo in pink on the side parked nearby.

Chris was looking around for her when she arrived. He was blond, clean-shaven, and wearing a tan leather jacket. He saw a pregnant lady in a short jacket and long skirt looking for someone as well. He had no idea that a beautiful, young black girl was next to her, ready to attack him if he was out of line.

"Hayley? I'm Chris. I ordered you a coffee. I hope that's okay?"

"I really shouldn't I try not to, being pregnant, but one won't hurt."

"When is he or she due?"

"It's a he, and he should be here in June, but who knows."

"So you want a baby shower cake for a boy? I've got my portfolio here if you want to have a look. I can bring you some samples if you like."

"No, it's fine. I think it's more about how it looks. I love this one. I like chocolate and yellow icing."

"You can decorate it with edible toys on top. Like blocks or a car. Or just have something written on the top like this one."

"I've got a thing for little bootees. Can I have a pair on top with blue ribbon? And 'It's a Boy' or something?"

"Perfect. Have you any idea how many people will be coming?"

"I only want a small one. We both have small families. And my friends aren't big cake eaters," she said, looking at Suzie.

"Here's my price list. That's for the smallest, for twelve people."

"That's fine. There's a lot of work in one. I could pick it up from you. Have you got a shop or premises?"

"Er, not anymore, unfortunately. I did until a few months ago. The overheads got too high."

"I'm sorry to hear that. Has business been slow?"

"I used to have three large orders a week and supply local shops and bakeries, but someone—I won't mention any names—ruined my business deliberately out of spite. But I have a feeling that things are going to get a lot better."

"Things could be worse. Did you hear about that baker in Little Beckles who actually got murdered yesterday? You're lucky."

"Er, I did hear something," he said nonchalantly. "I didn't know her, though."

"That's the first lie," said Suzie.

"Her name was Saloni. She made cakes as well."

"Really? It doesn't ring a bell. I'll write you an invoice. If you could just pay a deposit, please, Hayley. It's got my address on it. I work from home, and you can pick it up from there when I text you. I won't let you down."

"I know you won't, Chris. And I'll be wanting a christening

cake later in the year. That will be a bigger celebration at our local church."

"I can give you a reference. Here's a photo of one I did for the mayor's daughter."

"I love the white icing with the silver flowers. It's beautiful." Hayley felt very emotional all of a sudden. "I'm sorry. I can't wait till he's here and I can hold him."

"The time will go quickly. My girlfriend and I are hoping to have one soon. If business picks up. They cost an awful lot of money, I've been told."

"I know. For something so small, they cost a fortune."

"Worth it, though. I'm going to do everything I can to make my business a success again."

"Even murder, do you think, Hayley?" asked Suzie.

"More than likely," answered Hayley. "I mean, I'm sure you will, Chris. Are you sure you have time to finish the cake? I was trying to get in touch with you yesterday morning, around nine or ten. Were you busy?"

"Um, I don't remember. Oh yes. I'd turned my phone off and was at home catching up on some chores." Chris rubbed his nose, a sure sign he was lying. The saying about your nose growing when you lie had some basis, Hayley remembered.

But she didn't have time to drink her coffee as she received a text, so she paid her deposit, made her excuses to Chris, and said she'd be in touch. Tom had some terrible news and told her to ring him as soon as she could.

While Hayley was choosing her cake, Terry and Abigail were walking to May's Days. They were holding hands, and Abigail was telling him about the wedding that she had always dreamed of.

"Well, for a start, I wouldn't be making my dress or any of the bridesmaid's. I'd want to be pampered myself for a change.

Let someone else pin me. I'd have five bridesmaids—all friends. But I'd make sure that none of them were better looking than me—for the photos."

"That would be impossible, love."

"Aw, that's nice. And I wouldn't want you looking at them," she joked. "We'd be married in church, of course. By Reverend Pete."

"Would you be wearing white?"

"Of course! What are you insinuating? Well, maybe off-white," Abigail conceded. "I'm more interested in the honeymoon. Where would you be taking your bride?"

"Somewhere exotic, like Bournemouth."

"Bournemouth?" said a shocked Abigail.

"I was going to say Bognor Regis. Okay, Eastbourne."

"Are you kidding me? I was thinking about Bali or America. At the very least, Spain."

"That would mean flying. I don't fly."

"They have these things called planes now, Terry," Abigail said. "You'll be fine. We'll have plenty of gins before we board."

"I might go to Benidorm. That was very popular in my day."

"Well, even that is better than Bognor."

"Nothing wrong with Bognor. I used to go there every year," Terry persisted.

"We'll compromise and go to Benidorm." Although inwardly Abigail thought, *it's* my fantasy, I'm going to Las Vegas. "I bet May doesn't recommend Bognor."

"She's going to suggest all the expensive ideas."

"Well, it is a special day, Terry. I'm having second thoughts now, actually. I didn't know you were so penny-pinching."

"If that's what it takes to spend my life with you, I would have spent every penny I had. Shame we didn't meet when we were alive."

"I know. But it's funny to think that you would be the same age as my grandad."

Terry let go of her hand. "Well, that's a bit of a downer. I hadn't thought of that."

"So it's good we've met now, isn't it? Hayley would say it was meant to be. We're already like an old married couple anyway."

"That's true, Abi. You can be a bit … What's the word?"

"Loving?"

"No, nagging," said Terry as she slapped him playfully on his arm. "Remember when you first came, Abi, and you were bossy and told us what to do…?"

"Yes… and?"

"That's it. I was just remembering."

"Ha, thank you. We have a laugh, though. I think that's the most important thing in a relationship. In ours anyway."

"You do make me laugh, Abi. Even when you don't mean to. Give me a kiss before we go in and see what this wedding planner charges a fortune for."

"And it won't cost us a penny."

They enjoyed being nosy, looking around May Palmer's small office. Her business was above the bank in Great Billings. There wasn't a desk and chairs, but there were two sofas opposite each other with samples and catalogues on the coffee table between them. They wished they had Suzie there to do a search of the filing cabinets, but they didn't have to wait long before they heard the sound of keys at the door, and May Palmer came in, followed by a young couple.

Terry and Abigail sat on either side of them and felt like it was their wedding that was being planned.

"So, I'd just like to take some details if I could. It's Kirsty and Luke, is that right? And you're getting married next year?" asked May.

Kirsty said, "I know it's early, but we heard that places book up very quickly."

"The best venues do, yes. Have you got any ideas where you'd like it?"

"We want somewhere where all the guests can stay overnight, so there won't be any travelling for friends and family. So probably a hotel."

"There's a few venues that we recommend, but Micklebrook Priory is beautiful. There's fifty bedrooms and an amazing bridal suite, which can be yours from the day before. You can get married in the local church, which is only a few minutes' walk. Or in one of the Priory's large rooms, like the orangery or the Great Hall."

"That sounds amazing."

"But expensive," said a worried-looking Luke.

"Actually, it's not as expensive as some of the hotels. The Courtridge Hotel has just started doing them, and that is expensive. What is your budget? Only I charge a percentage."

"We have no idea yet. We don't know about most things. Have you got a list of all the things we have to do? I must admit I find it all a bit overwhelming. That's why we need a planner. We both have full-time jobs, so we need help. Luke's parents are expecting a big wedding, and my nerves and heart won't take all the stress."

"It is a very stressful time. I know one of the cake ladies I recommend told me that she was doing a wedding, and the actual bride died of a heart attack."

"Oh, God, we definitely need you then."

Terry whispered to Abigail, "That could be a motive for some poor bloke. I wonder if it was Saloni who told her."

"Or maybe the groom killed her. Tom should know about that."

"Now, after you've chosen the venue," said May, "you need to send out the save-the-date cards. There's no point having a wedding if a lot of your guests have booked a holiday. Then decide on the theme, and if you want a band or a disco. A good

DJ gets booked months in advance. So will the accommodation. Your guests will want to stay the night. But I can do all that for you. And I'll tell you when we need to book the cake and florists —usually about six months before the day, I would suggest. And don't forget all the legalities with the registrar."

"Oh dear," said Kirsty. "I'm even more worried now."

"That's what I'm for. You can just forget about everything. Even on the day, I'll be there to make sure everything runs like clockwork. You can ask for a reference from any of my clients."

Abigail grinned. "Maybe not Amelia Newberry."

Suddenly, there was a commotion from outside. The two ghosts and the three people all looked towards the window as a car outside was blowing its horn nonstop. Abigail looked down and saw a small red Mini was parked outside.

"Terry, it's Hayley and Suzie out there. We'd better go. Something bad must have happened!"

As soon as they got in the car, Hayley roared off as fast as the little car could.

"Where are you off to in such a hurry?" asked Abigail.

"I think there's been another murder."

Chapter 6

AFTER HAYLEY PICKED UP TERRY AND ABIGAIL, THEY drove to Bingford, where Tom told her he had been called to a suspicious death. He didn't say what it was, but going by the two police cars with flashing blue lights, she assumed it was a murder. Hayley saw Tom and called him over to the car while the others got out.

Tom's police constable friend, Jane Nichols, was consoling an old man, and Tom said Hayley had two minutes till Johnson got there, so they talked very fast.

"That poor man came back from a doctor's appointment and found his wife dead. He was only gone for half an hour, so we've got an accurate time of death for a change."

"Is it anything to do with the other murder?" asked Hayley.

"Well, she's not a cakemaker. Actually, she's like Abigail was; she's a dressmaker. Now go quick before the boss sees you and goes mad."

"Okay, hun. By the way, Abigail, Terry and Suzie are just going in to take a look."

"That's all I need. See you later, love."

"I'll do you something nice for tea."

"Don't wait up. I think I'm going to be late. Now go!"

At that moment, Abigail was looking at the crime scene. She told young Suzie not to touch anything or even look at the gruesome sight. An elderly lady was slumped over her sewing machine with a big gash in her back.

"Shame Lillian isn't here. But it looks like she died instantly, as there's not much blood. Struck in the back, straight through the heart, I reckon. It must have stopped beating straightaway." Abigail pointed to a pair of scissors on the desk next to the body that were red on the points. "That must have been what she was killed with. I wonder why they left them. She probably didn't even see who attacked her if she was working."

"You're right there," said a voice that they didn't recognise. "I was sitting there sewing the hem on that bridesmaid's dress when I felt a pain in my back and everything went black for a while. I thought I'd had a heart attack until I heard what you said. You think someone stabbed me in the back with that pair of scissors? And who are you three, and what are you doing in my house?"

"We're kind of dead detectives. And this is a coincidence, I was a dressmaker like you till I was killed. Then we solved my murder and try to solve others."

"Who knew sewing was such a dangerous profession? I knew I should have worked in an office. But I know this much: those aren't my scissors. I always use the orange-handled ones."

"Well spotted. Sorry, what is your name?"

"Miriam Bell."

"And they're new. Look, they've got the price tag on. He must have come in with them so you wouldn't have time to see him or her. The police would just think they're yours," said Abigail.

"My husband wouldn't have a clue. The killer must have forgotten to take the price off, though."

"That could be how your murderer is caught. I can hear the

inspector is here, Miriam. We don't like him at all. But the sergeant is nice."

Detective Chief Inspector Johnson felt a chill in the air. "Another day, another stabbing. If only everyone was as chilled and perfect as you and me, Mills."

"Very true, sir."

"Tell me who, what and when."

"I don't know much yet. It didn't happen long ago. This is Miriam Bell. Aged sixty-two, according to her poor husband out there that found her. She's a dressmaker who works from home."

"A pretty busy one, looking at all the clothes on racks."

"Didn't we have another dressmaker that was murdered about a year ago, sir?"

"Did we? Don't remember her," said Johnson.

Abigail was annoyed. "Well, that's just typical. Gone and forgotten. I was killed just like you at home."

"Do you think there's a connection?" asked Miriam.

"No, I don't, but there could have been. Dave Mills had the sense to think of it. I'm beginning to wonder if your murder is linked to a woman who was killed yesterday. She made wedding cakes. And you were sewing a bridesmaid's dress."

"But weddings are only a small part of what I do. Most of my jobs are for locals and a few shops," said Miriam.

"That's like me. I used to do Brooks in Becklesfield."

"I do them now. Small world. Well, I used to do them. Listen, that silly man is saying that they're my scissors."

"Don't worry, we have a living friend who can tell the young police constable that they're not yours."

"Look, sir," said Mills. "These have still got the price on. They must be new. Perhaps they weren't hers. The sticker says they're from a haberdashery in Gorebridge."

"Get the forensics to bag and tag, and we'll check them out tomorrow."

"If she was self-employed, she'll have a receipt somewhere. Uniforms can check."

"Yeah, they can check. Let's get out of the way. The forensics team and the doc will be here soon. I wonder if there's a pub close by."

"I believe the Cross Keys is the closest. We can walk from here."

"I can't be long, though, Mills," said Johnson. "I've got a date."

"Really?!"

"Don't sound so shocked, man."

But Mills was. "Should we talk to the husband first? He found the body."

"Is he off the hook yet?" asked Johnson.

"I was told he'd been for a doctor's appointment, so more than likely. And he doesn't look the guilty type to me."

"When do they ever? But I'll take your word for it."

WPC Nichols had led the distraught husband to a nearby bench and was sitting next to him, holding his hand. She stood up when she saw her boss coming.

"Sir, this is Brian Bell. He was the one who found his wife's body. This is DCI Johnson, Mr Bell."

"I'm very sorry for your loss, but I still have to ask some questions, sir. Can you think of any reason why anyone would do this to Mary?"

"Miriam," corrected Mills.

"No one at all. Everyone loved her. She wouldn't hurt a fly."

"Did you see anyone about when you got back? Or hanging around when you left?"

He put his head in his hands. "I can't remember if I did. My memory isn't so good these days. I don't think so. Who did this?"

Mills said kindly, "We'll find out, sir."

"One more thing, did you or your wife know someone called Saloni Kaye?" asked Johnson.

"I don't know. But my wife had a lot of customers who were always in and out at all hours. She would write them in her diary if that helps."

"Nichols, make sure we get her diary. Okay, sir, is there someone we could ring?"

"My daughter will come. I don't know her number offhand. Miriam would do all that. What am I going to do now?" Brian Bell broke down, and even Johnson felt pity for the old man who was now a widower.

Chapter 7

"Who would want to kill me?" asked Miriam for the third time.

"I don't know, hun." They had all come round to Hayley's to see what else they knew. "Come and sit down, Miriam. We'll find out, though. It must have something to do with the lady who was stabbed. It can't be a coincidence you were connected by weddings. Can you remember whose wedding you were working on?"

"It was three bridesmaids' dresses that needed turning up. I think the bride's name was Amy, no, Amelia."

"Well, isn't that a coincidence? Now we're getting somewhere. We're very good at what we do," Abigail assured her. "Hayley, you definitely have to go to that wedding now. Why don't we try the charity shop for your outfit? We'll go in the morning. You've got no excuse then."

"Okay. You'll have to come and help me choose, though. And it'll have to fit now you don't do my alterations anymore. I don't do sewing. You know that saying, 'A stitch in time saves nine'? Well, I let it get to at least twenty. And I know you'll say if it suits me. If nothing else, you're honest."

Terry added, "That's true, you're not exactly known for your tact."

"I'm very tactful, actually," Abigail said while blinking very fast. "I've been told how much tact I have on many occasions."

They all wanted to know by whom, but she was saved from answering as there was a flurry of activity and Betty burst in through the conservatory window.

"Miriam, I came as soon as I heard. Do you remember me?"

"Betty? I thought you'd died. Oh, so have I. It takes a lot of getting used to."

"I know, dear. But it's not as bad as you think it is. I'm having a bit of me-time before I join my John in the next part of the journey. But I'm in no hurry; he's not going anywhere, and we do have a lot of fun solving the odd crime or two, so you're in good hands."

"I'm not really worried about me. I'm quite happy to pass on. It's my Brian I worry about. I'm his carer; he suffers from Parkinson's. It's getting worse as he gets older, and he won't be able to live on his own. He could go and live with my daughter, but I'm so angry with whoever did this. I swear, I'll haunt them for life if I ever find out."

"We will," said Lillian as she put her arm around her. "I saw quite a few patients with Parkinson's when I was a nurse, and I'm sure he'll be okay. We can keep an eye on him and get him help if it's needed. Hayley knows a lot of people. So don't worry."

The phone rang, and Hayley answered it in the other room.

"Hi. It's Tom," he whispered. "Miriam was killed between two and three. The neighbours didn't hear a thing. But someone heard a van or a lorry because they thought it sounded like a diesel engine. The husband has Parkinson's, so the doctor said he probably wouldn't have had the strength to kill her. And he seems broken-hearted. She was his carer. Sometimes I hate this job."

"I know, hun. Did you see the scissors? Abigail noticed they were new. And they weren't bought by Miriam."

"How could you possibly know that?"

"Miriam told us."

Tom shook his head. "Of course she did. Okay, love, I'll see you tonight. Bye for now."

When Tom got home at nearly midnight, he found Hayley and Luna on the sofa, fast asleep. And he hoped there were no ghosts present. But he needn't have worried. Miriam had gone to see her daughter and check on her husband, and the others had returned to the Becklesfield Public Library.

The following morning, Hayley made her way to Wet & Wildlife, the charity shop that supported the flora and fauna in the local woods and the River Gore.

"You're late," said Abigail as soon as she saw her friend walking down the high street.

"It's alright for you. You don't have anything else to do. I still have to do the housework and feed the cat. You don't even have to have a shower or get dressed."

"Rub it in, why don't you," said Abigail, pretending to look upset.

"I'm sorry, hun. Take no notice of me. I'm just worried I'll look awful on the day in a cheap second-hand dress."

"Don't be daft. We're going to find you a beautiful outfit for this wedding."

"Never mind beautiful, Abi, I want to look thin."

"That ship has sailed, Hayl. I'm not a miracle worker."

"Tact, remember."

"Oh yes, you'll look beautiful and thin. Just like a supermodel."

"See. It's not that hard, is it?"

The Deadly Wedding

Mr Harding, the manager, said hello to Hayley and wondered why she was talking to herself. But he knew she was a bit eccentric. Someone said she was something to do with the paranormal. He also knew that she was married to a policeman. He had seen them together at The Cricketers on the night of the pub quiz when there was that ghastly murder.

"Is there anything I can help you with?"

"I'm going to a wedding, so I need something to hide this," she said, with her hand on her belly."

"He's not a magician, Hayley," laughed Abigail.

"Tact," she repeated. "Oh, sorry, Mr Harding, I mean that," she said, pointing to a dress on the front of a rack. "That looks nice." She had seen a black dress, with three-quarter-length sleeves and a high waist. Abigail said it did look nice and told her that black can be slimming.

"You can try it on at home if you like. Or go behind the curtain," said Mr Harding.

Hayley held it up against her and looked in the mirror. Even the length was good. Abigail pointed to a cream jacket and told her to take that as well, telling her that it would hide a multitude of sins—no offence.

"And I'll take this jacket. And I'll try them on at home. I've got a cream bag and shoes that will go perfectly."

"Make sure you keep the receipt then," he said as he put them in a bag.

"He means if you can't get them on," said Abigail with a grin.

"I'm sure they'll be..." Hayley went quiet as she saw a watercolour painting behind the counter. "That painting, is that for sale?"

"The one with the windmill? Yes, it is." He lifted it down and looked at the back. "It's quite expensive, though. It's not a print. It's an original. You can tell by the brushstrokes. I mean, it's probably just a local painter, not done by a master or anything, but it's still thirty pounds, I'm afraid."

"Have you got any idea who painted it?"

"It's signed by R. Raven. I can't say I've heard of him. If I remember correctly, it was part of a house clearance. I wasn't here at the time; one of my ladies took it. That was a few years ago. It's been hanging there ever since."

"I've been in here plenty of times and never noticed it before. Do you know who donated it?"

"No, I don't. Do you like it?"

"I don't know, but I'm going to buy it. Do you know where the windmill is?"

"No idea, but I'm sure someone will. Maybe one of the older people in Becklesfield. There aren't that many windmills around here anymore."

"Well, thank you very much for your help. I'll try the outfit on today."

Before Hayley reached the door with her purchases, something else caught her eye. It was an ornate oval mirror. The brass frame had lost its shine, and the glass itself was cracked at one of the corners.

"Where did you get this?" asked Hayley, without taking her eyes off it.

"I'm not sure. One of the other ladies must have accepted it. I probably wouldn't have in that condition. I can't see anyone buying it. Unless you're interested?"

"Er, no, sorry. But I would like to know its history."

"I'll see if I can find out. Are you alright? You look a bit pale."

"I think I've been overdoing it. I'm sorry to trouble you. Thank you, Mr Harding."

Abigail and Hayley left, and Abigail couldn't wait to find out what was wrong with her friend.

"What's up, Hayley? You saw something in that mirror, didn't you?"

Hayley took a deep breath. "Actually, it's what I didn't see, hun. It was awful. It turned me cold. I didn't see myself in the mirror. I didn't see the shop behind me. And I didn't see Mr Harding when he came over."

"I don't understand. What did you see?"

"I saw a room, not the shop. And a hazy mist. I can still see it in my mind's eye."

"Couldn't you just buy it? He said you could have it cheap."

"I don't want that thing in my house, Abigail. Ever. Especially with the baby coming. I don't know what it held, but there was evil in it. No, I don't want it in my house."

"Try and forget all about it. Hopefully, the dress will fit and you won't have to go back there. You didn't get the feeling of evil with the windmill painting, did you?"

"No, that was something else. I liked that."

Abigail couldn't wait to get back to Hayley's house and see if the dress and jacket looked good enough for the posh venue. But the outfit was thrown on a chair. Hayley only had eyes for the painting.

"Okay, Hayley, what's got you all hot and bothered? It's just a windmill and a stream on a cloudy day. The trees are blown flat, so I presume it's windy and the sails are going round, but that's all I see. It's hardly a Constable."

"That's all I see. But that's not all I feel. Actually, that's not true. When I first saw it, I saw a lady standing by the stream and pointing. But she's gone now."

"Ugh, spooky. I can't see anyone."

"There's a reason that I saw it today. It kinda called my name, if that makes sense."

"It wouldn't have done a year ago, but nothing would surprise me now about you, Hayley. You're amazing."

"Bless you, Abi. I think there's a soul or a spirit that I have to help. I bet Terry might even know who the painter is."

"Terry? Art? I don't think so. You'd be better going to see Janette at the library. She'd know. And if she didn't, she'd know what book to look it up in. We'll go now. But first, you need to try that dress on."

"Do I have to? I'm imagining I'm going to look gorgeous, and I'd rather not spoil the image in my head with the reality of looking like a big lump of coal. Oh, if I must. Look the other way then. Okay," said Hayley as she smoothed the dress down. "What do you think? And be truthful, hun."

"Hayley, you look…"

"Like a bell?"

"You look like a supermodel. Honestly, I'm not joking. I'd have tears in my eyes if I could. It falls from under the bust and hides a multitude of sins."

"Really? You like it?"

"Put on the jacket. Perfect. You won't be able to do up the buttons, but that won't matter. And you can take that off for the evening. It fits a treat. Would I lie to you?"

"No, you wouldn't. Is the length okay?"

"Perfect. Go up and look in your full-length mirror."

"Are you sure it's not too short?"

"You always hide your legs under those long skirts. You've got great legs. You look fantastic. Tom will be really shocked."

"Tact, remember. But that's a weight off my mind. I can concentrate on the painting now."

"What about the two murders, Hayl? That's more important."

"I'm not sure we can do much until Tom gives us some more suspects. The cake man and Saloni's husband have got an alibi, and they're still checking on where William Murphy was after he left work. And they still haven't found out whose dog was there at the time."

"And I can't think who would want Miriam dead. Dressmakers are the salt of the earth."

"If you say so, hun. So, shall we solve the mystery of the painting?"

"I do like a good mystery," said Abigail, rubbing her hands together.

Chapter 8

It wasn't very busy at the Becklesfield Public Library when Abigail and Hayley arrived. There was a young mother with a boy looking at picture books, and that was all. Even the other ghosts weren't there, apart from the ginger cat, Tiggy, who was wandering around. She was Luna's mother, who had died and led Abigail to find her kitten. Terry was in the churchyard checking for newly Deads, and Lillian had gone with Suzie to visit her brother and mother. As they walked together towards Janette, the head librarian, Betty came back from her daughter's house.

"Can you spare me a minute, please, Janette?"

"Of course, Hayley. Do you need another Train Your Cat book? Or has Luna calmed down a bit now?"

"Not particularly, no. I think I've given up on training him. I rather think he has trained me. Actually, I want to show you a painting I got from the charity shop." Hayley took it out of the bag and laid it on the counter. "I know you live in Windmill Lane, so I wondered if this was the one that was there?"

"Oh gosh. That was a long time ago, but it certainly looks like it. We moved there when I was four, so that's about fifty

The Deadly Wedding

years ago now. Our row of houses used to be the farmers' tied cottages. My dad was the foreman there, and when the farm was sold, we rented it and eventually bought it. I'll see if we have any photos of it in the local section. Yes, here it is. Sherrocks Windmill. Built in 1894 and became derelict in 1997 when it was demolished for safety reasons. What a shame they didn't preserve it. There's the stream that joins the River Gore further down. Yes, it's definitely the one. If you walk along the lane towards the river, you'll see where it used to be. The trees will still be there—just taller."

"That's great, Janette. I don't suppose you know the artist. Mr Harding thought that he might be local as well. I don't think it's worth anything. It looks a bit amateurish, doesn't it?"

"We've got a book about local artists and sculptors. Here we are. You might be able to work out when he painted it as well. Raven is an unusual name. Here it is. Oh, I was wrong. It's a her. Rowena Raven. This is another one of her paintings. Looks like it's of the Gore and sailing boats. This one was painted in 1987 and was in an art gallery in Gorebridge. So she was somewhat successful. Are you hoping that it's worth something?"

"Not at all. I need to know the history for another reason."

"Ah," said Janette knowingly. She knew from the talks that Hayley had given to the Women's Institute that she had psychic abilities. She had also seen them for herself in the past. "Do you feel there's something about this particular site? I won't say anything."

"I'm not sure. There is something that this painting wants me to know. But until I've learned everything about it, I won't know what that is. Does it say anything else about Rowena Raven? Is she still alive?"

"Hmm, she's dead, unfortunately. But she had a son, Jack, who was also an artist, if that helps."

"It does, thank you. I'll let you know if I find out anything else. As soon as I get the chance, I'm going to find those trees and that stream. Could I take out those books, please? I need to find out everything I can about the Raven family."

Betty and Abigail had found it very difficult to keep quiet as Janette was talking. But they waited until they were all walking towards Hayley's house again.

"How exciting, dear. It's the perfect paranormal puzzle."

Abigail agreed. "It's a real mystery. A haunted painting and a dead artist. And a woman that appears as a ghost by a windmill. It would make a good book."

"Don't remind me," said Hayley. "I keep putting off writing down our cases."

"Yes, you are a poor Watson. But never mind. This is far more interesting. Are we going there now?"

"I can't. Tom is finishing early today, and I've got to tidy the house. Do you want to come with us, Betty?"

"Do bears sit in the woods?" she answered. Hayley was glad Betty had got the saying wrong for a change.

"Can we go first thing tomorrow then?" pleaded Abigail.

"You know what they say, dear, never put off till today what you can do tomorrow, or something," Betty said.

"Sorry, Betty. I have got to put off till tomorrow today. I'm sure whatever is there can wait."

"I reckon someone was murdered there, don't you, Abigail?"

"Or had their head cut off by the windmill."

Hayley screwed up her face. "I do hope not. The last thing I want to see is a headless ghost. So we'll go tomorrow. But right now, I have a bed with my name on it. I'm going to put my feet up and have a look at these books. If the cat lets me!"

Luna, the tortoiseshell cat, had other ideas. He'd been left on his own far too much lately. He hadn't had his first lunch, let alone his after-lunch snack. And he hadn't seen that red light he had to chase for days. But he settled for a bowl of food and a cuddle on his double bed upstairs.

As much as she hated it at the time, Hayley was glad that Luna had walked on her face and hair and woken her up. It was dark, and when she looked at the clock, she realised that three hours had passed and Tom would be walking through the door at any minute. Luna always knew when he was due home somehow and sat on the front window in anticipation.

Hayley saw there was an old nail already in the kitchen wall and hung up her new painting. First of all, she gave it a wipe with a damp cloth, which turned brown with all the dirt and probably nicotine it had accumulated over the years. It looked at home straightaway. It was the first thing that Tom noticed as he walked in.

"That's nice. Is it new?"

"To us. But it was painted around 1987. I got it from the charity shop."

"Oh no, not more junk. I swear you take three things in and bring back ten. Mostly my stuff."

"Well, you keep your clothes till they fall to bits or are just old-fashioned."

"Rubbish. And last time I was in there, I saw the birthday present I bought you."

"As if I'd do that," said Hayley, as she thought of the awful yellow cardigan with the wooden buttons that she'd got rid of. "But you'll be pleased to know that I got a great outfit for the wedding. It would cost me ten times what I paid if I had got it in town."

"We're definitely going then, are we? That means I'll have to get my suit cleaned."

"You'll need a new shirt and tie, hun."

"Why? There's nothing wrong with my shirts. They're practically new."

"Tom, you're having a new shirt. And a new tie. I'll order you one. So what do you think of the painting?"

"It's quite nice. Is it worth anything?"

"It might be. I'm looking into it. It's painted by a local woman—Rowena Raven."

"Raven? That name rings a bell."

"She had a son called Jack. Could it be him?"

"Maybe. It'll come to me. Where's the windmill?"

"Just outside the village. I'm going there when I have the chance."

"Well, don't go on your own. You could fall or anything."

"Aw, are you worried about me?" Hayley went and sat on his lap. "I just about still fit."

"Blimey, you feel a bit..." He saw the look on her face. "...as light as a feather." But that was it—Luna wasn't having that. That was his lap, not hers. He meowed as loudly as he could until she moved, and he jumped up. That was more like it.

"Any news about the murders?"

"Not really. I feel so sorry for Miriam's husband. He's staying with his daughter for now. She's been sorting out that sewing. But this is a coincidence—Amelia's mother turned up while Jane was there and demanded she get the bridesmaids' dresses back. Two were done, but one was still in the sewing machine. Luckily, there was no blood on it. Anyway, Johnson said she could take them. If I'd have said I was going to the wedding, he'd have said no. He really hates you and me."

"I know. That's gratitude for all his cases we've solved. Anything else?"

"We know William Murphy left work at eight o'clock that morning, but he won't say where he was till he met Colleen. He said he drove around until it was time to go there. Now we've got to check where he was when Miriam was killed."

"She didn't see who it was. They already had the scissors in their hands and stabbed her. Johnson wouldn't have known they weren't her scissors if she hadn't told us."

"He still doesn't. How can I tell him that the dead victim told my wife they weren't hers?"

"Fair point, hun. You'll have to tell Dave."

"I don't know how, but I will. She's not still here, is she? Honestly, I'd have a heart attack if I saw an old lady with a pair of scissors sticking out of her back."

"Don't be silly, hun. The murderer didn't leave the scissors in her back. So you'd only see a red gash."

"Oh, that's alright then," he said sarcastically. "You will promise me that things like that won't be here for the baby to see. Not that he'll be able to, will he? Will he?"

"Of course not, Tom." But Hayley did worry about that. She knew her little boy would have the gift, the same as her. He would be able to see ghosts as easily as he could see his mummy and daddy. So she would have to make sure that he didn't see any gory sights. But Abigail and the others would help with that. They were already fiercely protective of her baby bump. And God help anyone that hurt her.

"Oh yes, Tom, just to let you know, I might have a baby shower. Or I might just have the cake. I haven't decided yet. So what do you want for dinner?"

"Don't change the subject. A baby shower cake? I know exactly what you're talking about. You went to see that bloke that shouted at Saloni, didn't you? The one from Cakealicious. Don't lie."

"Oh, was that him? I wasn't going to lie. I simply went to see him to find out how much one would cost. And I've ordered a very small cake. He was very nice, actually. So we'll have to have our parents over or something."

"Have you forgotten it's the wedding soon?"

"Damn. I'll have to find someone else to eat it," said Hayley, smiling.

"I bet you will."

"I am eating for two, hun."

"Just for two?"

"Cheeky. So is Johnson thinking the murderer of both ladies is the same?"

"He will if he can get an easy arrest with Murphy. But you never know with him. Now, if it was a candlestick maker, he might have done. You know—the butcher, the baker, and candlestick maker. Instead of the baker and the dressmaker."

"Oh yes. It's a wonder Abigail hadn't thought of that. You might be onto something, hun. We'll have to wait to see who's next."

"Are there such things as candlestick makers anymore?" asked Tom.

"Not as such. I suppose that goes back to the days before electricity. Candle makers, yes. There's hundreds of them. We should bear it in mind anyway."

"Not we. The police. It's not your case. You need to rest and stay away from all things murder."

"You're right. Tomorrow, me and my friends are going to have a leisurely walk by the river and see where the windmill in the painting was."

"So no investigating."

"A simple walk in the country, hun. There's no danger in that!"

Chapter 9

ABIGAIL WAS GETTING IMPATIENT SITTING AT THE kitchen table with Terry and Betty until Hayley came downstairs in her dressing gown.

"Was that the door? Come in," she said sarcastically and rolled her eyes. "Honestly, you lot, I could have been doing anything."

"Oh, we've seen everything anyway," snapped Abigail, until she saw Hayley's face. "Only joking. How do you feel this morning?"

"Huge and counting down the days. What's up with you today?"

"Oh, I don't know. I really feel for Miriam. I think it's because she was working her guts out like I used to, and someone killed her. And we have no idea who. If we don't solve this one, I might give up."

"We will, hun. It's early days. That William Murphy might be guilty. They've got to check his alibi for yesterday yet. But first, we've got to go to this wedding. I'm not looking forward to it at all. Will I even be able to get through the service without having a pee?"

Terry said, "You'll be fine. I'm more worried about what's going to happen there. You did foresee something. And we forgot to tell you, we heard May say that one bride had had a heart attack on the day of her wedding. That might mean something."

Betty said, "Could we forget about that for today? Terry, look, there's the painting."

"That's up along Windmill Lane. Well, it was. We used to hang out there when I was a lad. They said you get a funny feeling about it, Hayley."

"I do. Sometimes I swear I see a woman standing there if I stare at it long enough. She seems to be pointing at something. Look, I'll go and get dressed, and then we'll get going. We won't take the painting, I'll take a photo on my phone."

"It's so exciting," said Betty. "I wonder what we'll see."

But after the fifteen-minute walk there, they couldn't see anything. No ghost of a lady and certainly no windmill.

"Are you sure it's here, Terry?" asked Abigail.

"Yes, look, that's exactly where the windmill was. And that elm tree is the one that's painted. Even that bush is in the painting. Mind you, it's a lot bigger now."

"I don't know what I thought would be here," said Hayley sadly. "Other than a dead woman who needs me to do something for her. It is a bit of a letdown, isn't it?"

"There's that dog over there," said Betty.

Terry whistled, and they were all shocked when the Golden Retriever cocked his head and leapt across the stream towards them.

"Hello, boy. What are you doing here? Champ," he added after looking at his collar. "Good boy, Champ. Yes, I know you're a good boy, but get down."

Abigail joined in stroking him as his tail wagged like never before. "Bless him. What can we do, Hayley?"

"I'm not sure. I've never worked with a dog before. I suppose he should go into the light. Luna wouldn't like him at our house."

"Can't we keep him in the library, Terry?"

"Tiggy wouldn't like that much either. I suppose we could take him back, but I bet he'd much rather be with his master. Surely that painting wouldn't have been telling you about Champ. It's hardly life and death."

"Unless it's the lady in the painting's dog," added Betty. "To some people, animals mean more than humans."

"Let's see if we can get him into the light, and then I'll see if the feeling and the lady have gone. I can't see other people's lights. Can any of you?"

Terry said he could. "Over the years, I've guided people after they've died, so I know where it is. Come on, boy. Off you go. Go on, Champ. Go into the light." Champ just ran around excitedly.

"Oh, for Heaven's sake," said Abigail. "Hayley, pick up a stick and throw it." She picked one up and threw it to where Terry was pointing. Champ ran after it and was gone. "There, he's gone."

"Clever Dick," said Terry.

"Well, it takes a woman to work these things out," said Abigail.

"Huh. Takes a man to see the light, though. If it was left to you..." They stopped and turned as a man in a tweed jacket and trousers tucked into his boots walked towards them.

"Can you see me?" he asked.

"Of course, we're as dead as you," said Abigail, who always went straight to the truth.

"I don't suppose you've seen Champ, have you? He's my dog?"

Abigail put her hand over her mouth and whispered, "Uh-oh, you're in trouble, Terry."

"Why me?" he started to say. "It was ..."

"Will you two stop it," said Hayley. "We really are sorry, but we just helped him to cross over. If we had any idea that he was with you, we would never have interfered."

But luckily, the elderly man looked relieved. "You don't know how pleased I am to hear that. I didn't know dogs could go with us. I'd have gone years ago. He was my most loyal companion in life, and I wasn't going to leave him behind. So can I join him now?"

"Of course," said Hayley. "Do you know how to?"

"I've been seeing people go into a light for years, so yes."

Hayley said, "Oh, before you go, you haven't seen a lady standing here, have you? Wearing a pink and blue flowery dress?"

"Sorry, no. Okay, I'm off. See you on the other side." And the elderly man went along the riverbank towards the light that would take him to join Champ.

Terry said, "You're lucky, Abigail. And me, actually. Phew."

"I know. I thought we'd had it for a minute."

Hayley looked worried and said, "I'm thinking. Look, I'm pretty sure I didn't buy that painting to let a dog pass over. If it wasn't the place, maybe it's something about the painting itself. Let's go back and have a good look at the frame or something. Tom thought he'd heard the name Raven somewhere. Perhaps it's about her family."

"Ooh, that's even more exciting. It's like a treasure hunt, and we're finding clues. It's another one for the book—The Case of the Haunted Painting."

But despite holding it up to the light and going over it with a magnifying glass, they didn't find anything. That was until Hayley carefully pulled out the tacks and took the wooden back off, and then it all started to make sense. And it was more serious than they could have imagined.

Chapter 10

ABIGAIL COULDN'T HIDE HER EXCITEMENT AS THEY sat back down at Hayley's kitchen table. Her mood had vastly improved since they had found a letter folded up behind the painting. "Open it. Hurry up, Hayley."

"I am. I just don't want to rip it; it's very old. Don't get too excited—it might just be a receipt for whoever bought it."

"I bet it's a love letter," said Betty. "My John used to write me letters and leave them in the strangest places. Never in the back of picture frames, though. Is it a letter, Hayley?"

"It is, Betty." The letter was on good-quality paper from a writing pad, and it had been folded four times. Hayley carefully laid it out on the table and pressed it flat. Her smile faded as she saw the words and started to read them out loud.

"To whom it may concern, if you are reading this, then I am dead. My husband killed me. Please look after my baby girls for me. Pippa."

"Is that it? No last name?" said Terry.

"No, only Pippa. She was obviously terrified of him. And she would have thought it would have been found by now. If the painting was done in the eighties, the baby girls could be thirty or even forty by now."

"That's so sad," said Abigail. "Can you imagine what that poor woman went through? Why didn't she take the girls and run? I can never understand why they stay with a violent partner. I'd have got out ages ago."

"It's never that easy," said Betty. "Someone I knew was with a horrible man. He treated her like a princess when they first met, told her how lovely she was, but then he gradually stopped her from seeing her family and friends until she was totally dependent on him. Even told her what underwear to go out in and stopped her from wearing make-up. If she so much as looked at another man, she would fear for her safety. And she'd be in trouble if a man looked at her, like she was making him look. She stayed for ten years. I often used to see her with bruises on her neck or the tops of her arms. If she ever did try to leave, he would threaten to kill her or the children, even her parents. But she left in the end; her family hadn't forgotten her, even if he had forced them apart. And they waited till she felt strong enough to get out, and now he lives on his own with his own misery. I just wish he was locked up. So you shouldn't judge, Abigail."

Hayley felt this was personal to Betty. This person was known to her. This person was her daughter. When the time was right, Hayley would ask her if she wanted to talk about it. But not in front of the others.

"You're right, Betty. Battered wives aren't just battered physically. Men like that should rot in jail. Let's hope Pippa did leave and just forgot about the letter. Is that possible, Hayley?" asked Terry.

"It's possible. But I saw her in the painting. A tall lady with fair hair in a summer dress. She must have been pointing to the side of the painting that she slipped the letter in. Luckily, we got

The Deadly Wedding

there in the end. I wonder if we can find out who bought the painting?"

"Perhaps it still belonged to R. Raven," said Terry. "They kept it."

"No. Janette's book said she had a son called Jack; it didn't mention a daughter called Pippa. So it's someone who owned it at some point between now and the eighties. It may have even been commissioned for someone. The son might know. Rowena Raven's husband may even be alive. That book said that she had one painting in an actual gallery in Gorebridge, so we could go there and see what they know."

"Trouble is, her husband has got away with it. Well, Pippa's dead at any rate. There's not much we can do, dear."

"I saw the painting for a reason, though. I mean, I've been going in that charity shop for years, and it's been there for at least two. No, we've got to do something."

Abigail shrugged. "It's not like there's much to do for the wedding murders. We've got to rely on Tom and Dave doing boring police work for a while. I wonder if Tom could do a search on the artist's son. Could you ask him, Hayley?"

"I could, but he's not going to be pleased. It was bad enough when I told him that they weren't Miriam's new scissors, and he has to think of a way to tell the others. Honestly, he'll be old before his time at this rate."

"What did you say?" asked Abigail as her eyes widened.

"I said Tom was worried about explaining about the scissors."

"No, after that."

"I said he'll be old before his time."

"That's it. I've found the connection."

"To the painting?"

"No, not that. The connection between the stabbings. It's because of the label on the scissors."

"Tom told me it's from a haberdashery in Gorebridge."

"The murderer actually wants us to know. I'm not sure why yet."

"What are you going on about, you silly woman?"

"I'll ignore that because I know you can't help it, Terry. It's your age. Answer me this—what was the first murder done with?"

"An antique knife."

"And Miriam's?"

"Scissors," said Betty.

"Yes, but new scissors. Get it? Something old, something new..."

"Oh, my giddy aunt! Something borrowed, something blue. You've done it again, Abigail, dear. Don't tell me there's going to be two more murders."

"I won't, but there will be! As you always say, Betty, you can bet the dollar on your bottom on it. So now we have to work out if this helps us."

"Well, if you're right, hun, if, it will be something borrowed next. So what other person could be the target that has something to do with borrowing? Apart from the bride, of course."

"Well, when I was a best man in 1972, I hired a suit. We went to a posh shop in town, and we all wore the same. Even the shirts and bow ties came from them. Could it be a clothes shop?"

"And you hire a car," said Betty. "We had a white limousine for one of our daughters. Could be a chauffeur is going to die next."

"Hmm. But it's the weapon that's been the old and new. Unless a car is going to run someone down," said Abigail.

"That's very possible, hun. We can't sit about, though. Perhaps we should get hold of Amelia and see if it means anything to her. And find out what she's borrowing for the day. At the very least, we need to get a list of all the services she's going to use—from the cars to the florist."

The Deadly Wedding

"I do hope she's not using our one in Becklesfield. Mrs Merry has been doing weddings for the last twenty years. And she was a dear friend."

"There are hundreds of flower shops, Betty. The chances of her doing them are very small. But as we know, chances aren't always in our favour. I think I should pay a visit to Amelia as soon as I can and find out exactly who is on the danger list. Whoever Pippa is will have to wait till after the wedding."

Chapter 11

HAYLEY TURNED OFF THE ENGINE OF HER LITTLE RED Mini outside the thatched-roofed house in Featherbridge. Whether it was Daniel's money or Amelia's, they obviously had plenty of it.

"Nice," said Abigail. "I wonder who the Porsche belongs to."

"Must be Daniel's. How the other half live, eh."

"I don't think it's half. There's a lot more poor people about. Don't forget your pen and pad. You've got plenty of notes to take, and it makes you look a lot more intelligent."

"Thank you very much, hun. Are you going to wait here?"

"Er, what do you think?"

"Not a chance in hell. But I thought I'd try. Now, you are going to keep quiet, aren't you, Abi?"

"They'll never know I was there," she joked.

Daniel Templeton opened the front door, with a dog barking behind him, and he wondered who on earth this pregnant woman was. For a few seconds, Hayley could see the panic on his face, and then he relaxed. No, it couldn't be his baby, he thought. He hadn't cheated on Amelia for nearly a year. And even then, he'd been careful. He didn't want to go through that again.

"Can I help you?"

"My name is Hayley. I'm an old friend of Amelia's. She invited me and my husband to your wedding to check a few things out."

"Oh, the psychic. She did tell me. I'm a great believer. Come in, please. Amelia, your friend Hayley is here."

A worried Amelia joined them in the vast hall. "Max, quiet. Get in your basket. Is everything okay, Hayley? Nothing has happened, has it?"

"Something has, but I'm not sure it affects you much."

"Come and sit down."

"It's a beautiful house. Oh, I'm sorry, are you expecting company for lunch?" said Hayley as she pointed to a table set for six.

Danny answered, "No one exciting. Just the parents coming round to talk even more about the wedding."

"I won't stay long, I promise. It's just that we—I mean I—need to ask you a few more things about the wedding. Did you hear about the other lady that was murdered in Bingford yesterday?"

"I did. It's dreadful. But I didn't know her. Miriam someone, I heard."

"Are you sure you didn't know her? She's a dressmaker, and I think she was altering your bridesmaids' dresses."

"The old lady in Belle Bridal? I didn't know her name. I think she went in when they had fittings that needed pinning. She's already done my dress, thank goodness. I didn't take much notice, I'm sorry to say. She was simply the one with the tape measure around her neck and the pin cushion on her wrist. That sounds awful now. I didn't even really look at her or ask her what her name was. Poor woman. But that hasn't got anything to do with us, has it?"

"I hope not, hun. But there does seem to be a pattern going on here. Both victims had something to do with weddings. It could be a coincidence that they both have a connection to you. But after what I said all those years ago, I'm not so sure."

"Oh my God, why is this happening to us? It's terrifying."

Abigail cut in, "Tell her about the something new."

"A friend of mine wondered if the old saying for luck—that you have to have something old, something new, something borrowed, and something blue—might be relevant. It might not be so lucky for someone. Starting with the old knife that was used in the first killing. We could be wrong, but just in case, could you tell me what yours are?"

"Blue is easy; I've got a garter. Something old; I'm definitely wearing my great-nan's silver necklace. New; I've got plenty." Amelia looked at Danny and smiled. "Including a very expensive pair of designer shoes."

"And if she thinks they're expensive, then they must be," he added.

"Something borrowed; I haven't made up my mind yet. Your mum—that's Fiona—wants me to wear her pearl earrings. They're really nice but a bit old-fashioned, but I'd like to start off married life with her on my side. I always get the feeling that your family thinks I'm a bit of a snob."

"Rubbish, they think the world of you."

"When you're around, she's as nice as pie, but not so much when it's just us two."

"My mother hasn't got a bad bone in her body."

"See, you always take her side."

Hayley didn't want to be the cause of a break-up, so she asked if there was anything else she might borrow for the day.

"My sister, Charlotte, wants me to borrow her diamante bracelet. It would go beautifully with my dress, but I don't want to. It didn't bring her much luck."

"Why's that?"

"She bought it for her own wedding, but Jason called it off with two months to go. I can't say I blame him."

"That must have been hard for her. Don't you get on?"

"Typical sisters. We got on well till we got to our teens, then it was war. She was always jealous of me."

"Is she younger?"

"Only by two years. I'm surprised you don't remember her from school. She was always trying to hang around me."

Hayley got up and went to look at the photographs on a shelf. "She looks like you."

Danny said, "Not as beautiful, though." Hayley looked into his eyes and caught a flash of guilt. Had he had an affair with the sister?

"Who are these? Are they your sisters that are the other bridesmaids, Danny?"

"Yes, my stepsisters, Eve and Ava. And that's their dad, George. It's very complicated. When Amelia first told me of a premonition that something was going to go wrong, I thought it might be something to do with the top table."

"Oh God, yes. It's a bomb just waiting to go off, Hayley. Let me see if I can explain. My father, the colonel obviously, was married before and had a family, but his wife isn't coming, only his daughters. Danny's mum is on her second marriage, so Danny's real dad, Tim, will be there with his wife, who doesn't get on with Danny's mum or his stepdad. What could possibly go wrong?"

"It must be a long table."

"I just thought, did you say that woman was doing my bridesmaids' dresses? Will we be able to get them back in time?"

"You will. I'll check to make sure. You might not know, Danny, but I'm married to a policeman."

Hayley saw a slight frown on Danny's brow. "Are you? I didn't know that."

"What do you do for a living, Danny?"

"Freelance marketing. I help companies to start up, so I'm travelling here and there most days. Is there anything else? We have got a lot to do. I'm staying at Monty's, my best man's house, on Friday night, and Amelia will be in the bridal suite at the Priory, so we need to start packing. Plus, the olds are due any minute."

"That reminds me, Amelia, could you give me a list of the other services you're going to use? Just in case they're targets."

Amelia went into the kitchen and came back with a white folder. On the front was May's Days. "It's all in here."

"Did May suggest all the services you're using?"

Danny said, "Not for me. We're getting the suits that my friends and I are wearing as best man and ushers from a bespoke tailor in London. Nothing to do with her."

"What about the others?" asked Hayley, as she got out her pad and pen.

"I think they were all because of her. Well, I've had to go to Cakealicious now to get a new cake. Luckily, he can fit me in at short notice—he had some cancellations. And he apologised for what happened at Saloni's. There are the cars from RC Limousines. The invitations and the favours were through May. The photographer was on her list—Philip Gowdy Photography. The caterers are the ones that the Priory always uses. And May will be there on the day. That's part of the service: to help with the timings and staff."

"Hairdressers?"

"I thought you knew that Mummy owns a chain of hairdressers called Flicks. Charlotte works in the Stonecroft one—when she bothers to go in."

"Does she? That's handy to know. I might go myself before the weekend. I had no idea. What about the flowers?"

"Ah, May had a few on her list, but I chose this one because

Mum uses them. It's a small florist in Becklesfield. Oh, you might know them then."

"Do you mean Mrs Merry, in the High Street?"

"Yes, that's the one."

Hayley and Abigail looked at one another. "I'd better get going, hun. Thanks for all the info."

"You don't think someone would kill us, do you?"

"No, hun, I'm sure they wouldn't."

"You're still coming to the wedding, aren't you?"

"Absolutely. I've even managed to get an outfit that doesn't make me look huge. Oh, I haven't got a hat, though. Will it matter?"

"No. Some are. Our mothers are, for the church of course. Most of my friends will be wearing fascinators. But it's totally up to you."

"I might wear my hair up and put something in it." Hayley had already decided that she needed to get a trim. And Charlotte in Stonecroft would be the perfect person to book. "Okay, if I don't see you before, I'll see you at the church."

As they got up, the doorbell rang, starting Max barking again. "It's our parents. For goodness' sake, don't mention anything to them. Especially Mother; she's panicking enough as it is."

"I won't, Amelia," promised Hayley.

She could tell straight away who the colonel was—they always had bushy moustaches. Mrs Newberry looked like a hairdresser, as not one hair was out of place, and Fiona was the spitting image of her son.

George came in last with a bottle. "Hello, all. Can't forget the Merlot."

After a quick introduction, Hayley made her excuses and got in the car.

Abigail was worried. "Right, quick, let's go straight back to Becklesfield and check on Mrs Merry."

ANN PARKER

But they were just too late.

Chapter 12

THE FIRST THING HAYLEY AND ABIGAIL SAW WAS AN ambulance, and Betty looking agitated and holding onto Terry's arm.

"I really hope you're wrong, Terry. Maybe Mrs Merry has just had a fall," said Betty. "She is getting on a bit. I wish Hayley and Abigail would hurry up."

"They'll be back soon," said Lillian. "Here they are now." And the spirits ran over to her car.

"The ambulance has just got here, Hayley. We think it's for Mrs Merry."

Hayley got out of the car to have a better look. "We think it is too, hun. We found out she's on Amelia's list to do her bouquets and centrepieces. It can't be a coincidence. Have you heard if she's still alive?"

"We were just going in to see," said Terry.

"I'll come too. I hate waiting," said Abigail. "Suzie, you stay here with Hayley."

They returned to the car in five minutes to let them know what had happened.

"How is she?"

"Not dead, thank goodness," said Lillian. "But she's been strangled. Looks like she was out the back making up an order of bouquets, and someone attacked her. The girl that works with her came back, and when the bell tinkled on the door, her attacker ran out the rear. She's unconscious, and they think she banged her head as she fell."

"She was very lucky," said Terry. "Looks like you might have been wrong about things, Abigail. You don't borrow flowers."

"Tom thought it could be another saying," said Hayley. "The butcher, the baker, the candlestick maker. Or, in this case, the florist, the baker, and the wedding dressmaker."

"Sounds more likely," said Terry, as Betty nodded in agreement.

"I was sure I was right," said Abigail glumly. "We had the old and the new. It was all making sense. So what was she strangled with, Lillian?"

"With a two-inch floristry ribbon that was on a rack."

That cheered Abigail. "Ah. And what colour was it, m'lord?"

"Oh, God, blue," Terry said begrudgingly.

"I rest my case," said Abigail. "Like someone once said—I had all the right notes, but not necessarily in the right order."

"So it must have something to do with Amelia's wedding. Abi and I got some more suspects today. We'll catch you up later," Hayley told them.

Abigail added, "I wouldn't be surprised if the murderer was planning to do the last killing on the day of the wedding. If they want to spoil her preparations this badly, they will definitely want to ruin their day. I couldn't really take to Danny, could you, Hayley? It could be him that's the target. Or the murderer, I suppose. We've got less than a week to work out who."

"No, there's something about him. He's got a lot of secrets."

Tom arrived as the paramedics were bringing out the florist on a stretcher. He had a quick word with them as they put her in the ambulance. He saw Hayley, but he didn't have time to talk to her, even though she was waving frantically. She would have to wait. Johnson and Mills had left Gorebridge Police Station at the same time as him, so he couldn't be seen talking to his wife. Tom put up the yellow tape and waited for the forensics team to arrive. He heard a car door slam hard and knew that Johnson was there. He was the only one who could slam a door that hard.

"Good afternoon, Tom. Hope you are okay. I see your wife looks blooming. You'll have to tell me what gift you want when the baby arrives."

Tom could only mumble and look at his friend, Dave Mills, who just shrugged. Surely he wasn't drunk already. He didn't look it. Mills was confused as well. He had actually heard Johnson humming as he walked to the car. He could only think that his boss had something evil planned for some poor unsuspecting person.

"So who is the unfortunate victim, Bennett?"

"Marcia Merry, a florist. She's a widow. In her sixties, I would guess. She's the owner of the business and was attacked out in the back workroom. We'll need to ask around to see if the attacker came in the front. He or she definitely left the back way. The paramedics think she'll be alright. But she is out for the count, so she can't tell us anything yet, sir."

"Right. What beautiful pink flowers. What are they?" Johnson asked as he smelled them.

"I think they're carnations, sir."

"Are they really?"

Tom had to ask, "Are you feeling okay, sir?" He was beginning to think that one of Hayley's spirits had taken over his body.

"Never better, son. So she was strangled by this ribbon?"

"Yes, sir. The forensics are on their way."

"Next of kin?"

"She lives with her sister at the other end of the village. I could tell her if you like. I know her quite well." This was when Tom expected him to say that it wasn't his job and to get back to keeping the locals out.

"Good idea. You do that. Give her a lift to the hospital if she needs one. You better stay with the old dear until she wakes up. She might have seen something."

Tom looked at Mills, and Mills looked at Tom in confusion. Tom thought he must have had too much whisky at lunchtime. Not that he could smell it. Perhaps he had switched to vodka. They say that doesn't leave a smell.

But Mills had a different take on Johnson's strange behaviour. He had seen the signs in some of his friends. He had even suffered from it himself. He never thought he'd live to see the day, but hadn't the inspector mentioned a date? That must be it. Detective Chief Inspector Johnson was in love!

"It's freezing in here," said Johnson, rubbing his arms.

"Probably to keep the flowers fresh, sir," said Mills, not aware that Abigail and Terry had joined them at that moment to learn what had happened.

"So who found the body, Tom? Wasn't your wife again, was it?" he asked jovially.

"No, sir. She was just passing and saw something was happening. We live here in Becklesfield."

"Do you? I never knew that. A nice village, is it?" Tom had never heard him take an interest in anything, especially not him. "But we better get on. Who did find the poor old woman?"

"The part-time girl, Ellie Bird. She'd gone to the village shop to get some sandwiches for their lunch. When she got back, she came in the door, and it slammed behind her, like it does when there's a draught from the back exit being open. The bell on the top of the door jangles, so that's probably what scared him or her off. Then she walked out here expecting to see her boss making up bouquets or putting the kettle on, but she was on the floor over there. The ribbon was around her throat and was still joined onto the rack. And there was blood from a wound on her head. She wasn't sure if it was a freak accident at first. But then she saw how tight the ribbon was and the mess everywhere, and she rang 999. She didn't see anyone. You can't get in the back way; you have to be let in or come in the front."

"Good point, Tom. Unless they knocked and she let them in. We'll have a look out there in a minute. Do we think it's connected to the other attacks? Or could someone have been after money? We'll have to ask the girl to check the till, but it doesn't seem likely. There's a post office two doors up if they needed cash and were prepared to use violence," Johnson pointed out.

"Very true," said Mills.

Johnson smiled at Tom, which, for some reason, unnerved him. "You get off, Tom. Pick up the sister and take her to see Mrs Whatsername and stay there till she comes round. And tell young Jane Nichols to talk to the locals. If they came in the front way, they must have waited till the girl left. Someone must have seen something. Keep me posted from the hospital."

"Will do, sir." Tom couldn't believe how nice Johnson was being today. It was like being in a parallel universe, so he left quickly before the spell was broken.

Mills and his boss went out the back. They found a narrow passageway that ran past the rear entrance of all the shops in the high street. "Where does it go, Dave?"

"This way to the church—there's the steeple—and the other to the pub," expecting Johnson to suggest a swift pint.

"No time for that today. They could have gone either way. Get forensics to check for footprints when they get here."

Abigail pointed to a pink carnation petal that was on the path leading to the church and then another one close by that must have been stuck to the attacker's shoe. "They'll miss them, look. They might blow away, and there's nothing we can do about it." But luckily, Mills saw them.

"Inspector, look—there's one of those carnations you liked. And another one."

"Well done, Mills. We'll make you an inspector yet. Make sure no one comes along here till the forensics have been. I've got to do something."

"At the Cricketers, sir?"

"Me? No. I'm going to get that girl to check if anything is missing and then get her to make me a nice bouquet. See you back at the station."

Mills shook his head. What on earth was happening?

Chapter 13

"I THINK WE CAN ALL AGREE THIS IS THE BIGGEST mystery we have ever undertaken," said Abigail at the meeting of the agency at Hayley's house.

"Agreed, hun."

"I, for one, won't rest until we know," added Betty.

"I'm in shock," said Lillian.

A hush came over the conservatory as they all thought about the enigma.

Terry spoke first. "I just can't think. Who the hell would be going out with Johnson?"

"And does she love him back?" said Abigail.

"Are you sure you all heard right?"

"As sure as I'm standing here, Hayl. He said he wanted to buy some flowers for her. And he was being nice to everybody. And—you won't believe this—he didn't even want to go to the pub. I swear on my life."

Betty said, "Love can make you do strange things. As you know, my John liked some strange things, especially in the ..."

"It sure can," replied Abigail quickly. Betty and John had a very colourful love life, right up till he died. The eighty-two-year-old always put the young ones to shame. And Betty was not ashamed to tell them all about it if they didn't watch out.

"I say we follow him and see where he goes and what he gets up to. He'll never know."

"Abigail Summers! You'll do no such thing. I'll get Tom to get to the bottom of it."

"Ooh, that reminds me, John loved to be ..." started Betty.

"Thank you, Betty. I think we've heard quite enough of John's bottom," laughed Hayley. "It's very sudden, though. He was his normal miserable self the other day. Maybe he met someone last night. Or maybe he proposed last night, and the poor woman said yes. Sorry, I shouldn't be wicked. But he's so nasty to Tom sometimes. But we'd better get on with Mrs Merry's attack. I hope she's okay. It must be to do with the other two? But who could it be?"

Abigail was in her element once more. She stood up and paced the room. "Okay. It must all be connected. But is it because of Amelia and Danny, or is that just a coincidence? There must be a lot of couples who are using all three services. Or could it be that someone needed one of them dead and wanted to muddy the waters? I'm going to discount Mrs Merry for now. She's not the type to make enemies, and she has no family waiting to inherit. And she's a sweet old thing. The same for the dressmaker. As you know, us dressmakers are very popular," said Abigail with a smile. "So I think the real target someone wants to hide is Saloni Kaye. Now, what do we think are the motives?"

"Not revenge," said Hayley. "I can't think anyone would want to risk their freedom for a cake. Although Chris lost a lot more than a couple of orders. He lost his premises and a lot of money, and he could have gone bankrupt. We need to find out if it was Saloni that did that to him. But she was doing fine on her own anyway. Apparently, she was even thinking of giving up weddings—too much trouble. Love? I'm not seeing that either."

"A drug deal gone wrong. Money?" said Betty.

"Tom said the husband had a thriving business. And their house is nice, but I can't see that anyone would gain anything by killing her, hun."

"Could be a reason that we've seen before," said Abigail. "She knew or saw something and had to die. Or the killer thought she knew something. Might not have anything to do with weddings or cakes."

"I think it has," said Terry.

"Oh, yes! I think you're right, Terry," said Abigail excitedly. "Bigamy!"

"You shouldn't swear, dear. It's not that much of a surprise that Terry is right."

"Bigamy, Betty! Biga, not bug ...."

"Oh, Betty," giggled Hayley. "You are adorable. You'll have to tell us what you mean, Abi."

"I think she was doing the cake for one of the couples, and one of them—the bride or groom—was already married. Perhaps she had done their original wedding. It could have already happened, or was going to in the future."

"Brilliant, hun. I think we can rule out Amelia. Tom can check Danny. Or we can at the library. He's only in his twenties, so it shouldn't take long. Obviously, if it's someone else and it happened years ago, that's a bit different."

"We'll have to look at the cakes she's got on her books now and ones she's done in the past few years. It could even have been when she was working in the bakers in Gorebridge," said Abigail.

"Tom's going to be busy. He found out that she began working for the bespoke company about ten years ago and started up on her own about two years ago. What about that one who was at the house that day? William someone. He got there before his partner did. They had met her the previous week, so it was their second appointment. He could have remembered her. He had means, motive, and opportunity."

"Yes, I think I'm right," said Abigail. "What? I don't always think that. Well, maybe sometimes. It could well be William Murphy. He didn't look as happy as her that he was having a big fancy wedding. And he didn't hear the dog, remember? It should be easy to check, as long as he's using his real name. So, what's the plan, Hayley?"

"I'm staying here until Tom gets home. He'll be here in a few hours, and I'll tell him everything. Hopefully, he'll say that Mrs Merry is alright. She might even know who attacked her."

"And you need to rest," said Lillian. "And from now on, you're not going anywhere without your bodyguard. Suzie may be small, but she's a match for anyone who has a go. It's dangerous out there. And she's the only one of us who can save you."

Abigail said, "Yes, Lillian's right. Especially as you said you're going to make an appointment at Flicks with Charlotte to have your hair done. I don't like to think that she'll be behind you with a pair of scissors after what happened to Miriam."

"Who's Charlotte, dear? Is she a suspect?"

"Oh yes, sorry, Betty. With all the excitement, we forgot to tell you what happened at Amelia's, didn't we, Abigail?"

"Johnson's love life threw us. Charlotte is her sister, who was jilted—not at the altar, but a few months before. So it could be anger that Amelia is having the dream day that she wanted. They don't get on, so could she have done all this to ruin Amelia's day? If so, I bet she's planning on doing something on Saturday as well. And funnily enough, she wants her sister to wear something borrowed from her—a diamante bracelet. So jealousy could be her reason for sure. We didn't think much of Danny either, did we, Hayley?"

"No. I had the feeling he was a bit of a cheat. Something else I need to ask Charlotte about. She's a hairdresser at her mum's firm. And we met their parents, who arrived for lunch as we were leaving. Which reminds me—nearly everyone at that wedding is remarried."

"There are going to be more steps there than at St Paul's Cathedral," added Abigail. "Stepmums, stepdads, and stepsisters and brothers. The top table is a bomb waiting to explode. Let's hope not literally. We can't do much till Tom gives us an update. Can you come to the library in the morning, Hayley, and tell us?"

"I will, hun. Now you lot go and do whatever you do. I'm going to have a nice, relaxing bath. But first, I must ring up Flicks and make an appointment with Charlotte to get me ready for the wedding, which I apparently said was going to be the talk of the county."

Chapter 14

HAYLEY GOT TO THE LIBRARY EARLY, BEFORE IT GOT too busy. Suzie was very excited about going to a real hairdressing salon. The nine-year-old had never been to one in her life. A friend of the family had always done hers and her mother's at their house.

"Luckily, I got an appointment for twelve o'clock this morning. But I've got so much to tell you from Tom. First off, Mrs Merry is going to be fine. She'll have to stay in for a few days as she has a mild concussion, but thankfully, she just has a few bruises from falling. She could have broken a hip or anything, so that's good news. But not so good is that she doesn't remember anything about the attack."

Lillian said, "That's usually the case with a head injury. It's often temporary, though."

"Also, you remember William Murphy, the reluctant groom. Well, it seems he was more reluctant than we thought. He's done a runner. So Johnson thinks he's guilty, so he's not bothering to look into it so much. Apparently, he's taking two days off. Personal leave."

"Do we know who the unlucky lady—I mean, lucky lady—is yet?" asked Terry.

"No. And it's not for the lack of the everyone trying to find out. I don't know why it's such a secret. But we'll know soon enough, probably."

"Did you tell Tom about the bigamy theory?" asked Abigail.

"I did. He's going to check out everyone. Saloni had detailed notes of names and what sort of cake they wanted since she worked for herself. And I told him he needed to check Charlotte and Daniel's alibis for the attacks. But he can't just ask—that's the trouble. Daniel doesn't work from an office, so he could have been anywhere. And Tom did say it seems an awful lot of trouble to go to if you wanted to stop the wedding, which is true. I didn't dare tell him that I've got an appointment with Charlotte today. He'd think I was taking chances again. I'll try and see where she was yesterday if I can."

"If I'm right about the murderer being a bigamist, there won't be any more murders. Not before and not on Saturday. For one thing, they won't be there, and also, the more murders you do, the more potential clues you'll leave. Plus, that would narrow the guilty one down to someone from the Newberry wedding."

"Thank goodness, because I'm really looking forward to it. Tom and I don't do much socialising these days. And this is probably the last time that we don't have a baby with us, so we can let our hair down. Not that I can drink, but I can have a bit of a dance."

"That's what I said to Terry. None of our dates so far have included a band. Actually, we can all have a dance."

"John and I loved to boogie."

"So we heard, hun. Come on, Suzie, girl's day out—just me and you."

Suzie and Hayley had not imagined Flicks was going to be quite as grand as it was. Hayley thought she probably should have checked the prices first. But how much could a wash and trim be?

"So, what are we doing today?" asked the stylist after Hayley was shown to her seat.

"I'm going to a wedding on Saturday, and I need to have a few inches off the length and ask your opinion about what I could do with it. Something fancy, but something I can do myself on the day."

"Ah, Hayley, Amelia's friend. I'm Charlotte. She said you might come."

"She recommended you."

"Really? That doesn't sound like my sister."

"Well, she knew I was desperate. Sorry, I didn't mean it to sound like that."

"I can see what you mean. Who cut it last? Your gardener with a pair of rusty shears?" Charlotte said, holding up the long black hair.

"I can't even remember. I just let it grow and then hack a bit off the bottom myself."

"It's as straight as a poker as well, isn't it? So you need to do something. This is the social event of the century, apparently," Charlotte said sarcastically.

"So I heard. Honestly, I don't know why she's bothering. All that money down the drain. And half of marriages break up these days."

That pleased Charlotte. "Exactly. I don't know if you know him, but I can't see it working between them."

"I met him once. And actually, I don't know your sister very well either. I think I'm there to make her look more popular. As if to say, she's so nice that she's still got friends from school."

"That sounds just like Amelia. Always how things will look."

"What do you think of him? I thought he seemed a bit shifty. I wondered if he'd ever cheated on her. He looked like the type to me."

Charlotte looked around and whispered, "Danny tried it on with me once."

"No! How could he?"

"It was at a family do. Mum's fiftieth at the Winston Hotel. We were a bit drunk, I'll give him that. I was outside the front, having a cigarette, and the next thing he came up behind me and put his arms around me. He told me I looked ravishing and we should go up to one of the rooms. He said, 'I've always fancied you, little sis'."

"No! That's awful."

"Of course, I told him to get lost. I might not be that lucky with men, but I didn't want my sister's seconds."

"Was he annoyed?"

"No. Laughed and said he was only joking. I knew he wasn't. I'd seen the way he looked at girls. And the way some of them looked back."

"Did you tell Amelia? I take it you didn't."

"I nearly did. But I decided to wait till after the wedding. Revenge is a dish best served cold, don't they say? Or I may even tell her on the day. But I'm looking forward to the evening, so who knows? I might get off with the best man."

"I don't think your parents will be too pleased either if you ruin the wedding day. I have great faith in karma myself."

"That's very true. It's all Mum talks about. She loves Daniel like a son as well. Mum hasn't liked any of my boyfriends. Mind you, usually for good reason. Is that enough off the bottom?" Charlotte said, holding up a mirror.

"Perfect, thank you. Could you blow-dry it and put a few curls in it?"

"I'll try. It'll take a lot of mousse and spray, though."

Hayley tried to think what Abigail would ask, but Suzie had a good suggestion.

"Did you hear that a florist was attacked near to where I live? You don't feel safe these days, do you?" asked Hayley.

"Well, the lady that was turning up my bridesmaid's dress was actually murdered. Stabbed with a pair of scissors."

"Oh, my God. How awful. Do you know who did it?"

"No idea. But the one that was doing Amelia's cake was killed as well. You've got to laugh, haven't you?"

Hayley thought not, but said, "It is funny, that's for sure."

"I know. Someone is trying to tell her something. Maybe it's one of Daniel's exes."

"I hadn't thought of that. I'm very impressed, Miss Marple. Or someone that really doesn't like her. I wonder what the police think," said Hayley.

"They questioned Amelia and Mum because they'd been there when a bloke threatened Saloni Kaye. I think it's Daniel trying to get out of it myself."

"Couldn't he just tell her it's over? A murder seems a bit over the top."

"I didn't say he wanted to finish with her. I'm not being snobby—well, maybe a bit—but his family is rich, but not as wealthy as us." Or maybe he's already married, thought Hayley, and doesn't want to be a bigamist.

Charlotte carried on, "And Amelia earns about four times what he does. Also, I'd already cancelled a wedding at the last minute. Perhaps he couldn't face the backlash of it being his idea. You don't know Daddy—ex-army. After my breakup, he said to Daniel if he so much as hurts a hair on her head or a beat of her heart, he'd get his old service revolver out. I think he meant it. Daniel wasn't quite so cocky after that."

"I bet. Let's hope the day goes off without a hitch. Sorry about the pun."

Suzie chuckled. "Abigail would like that."

"I'm surprised you're working this week. I would have thought you'd have been given the week off for your sister's wedding."

"I have got it off. It's just that Mandy has Wednesdays off, so I had to come in today."

Hayley stopped with the questions to have a proper look in the mirror. "I love it, Charlotte. It's amazing what a few curls can do. My hair looks twice as thick."

"You need some sort of product to give you body."

"Can I have some, then?" said Suzie, giggling.

"Very good, hun. I mean, it's good to know, Charlotte."

"I bet you've had the same style since you were five."

"That's where you're wrong. I had a fringe till I was eleven."

"It did look a bit witchy, if I'm honest, Hayley."

"I never mind a bit witchy, Charlotte. Any ideas for Saturday? I'm wearing a black dress and a cream jacket."

"Hmm, keep it down, I think. If you're not used to putting it up, it will never last the day. If I were you, I'd put it all to one side, just behind your ear. In a ponytail like this."

"Wow. It actually suits me. Even I could do that."

"You look lovely, Hayley," said Suzie.

"Use a black band or a cream scrunchie and then push a cream flower in. An artificial one would be best. You don't want it to wilt or the petals to fall off in your dinner. Unless you're thinking of wearing a hat."

"Definitely not. The only hats I own have bobbles on. I'm so pleased with what you've done, Charlotte. Thank you. I'll make sure to add a good tip."

Charlotte took off the cloak and shook it, all over Suzie. "You can pay at the desk. I'll see you on Saturday, then. Let's hope it all goes according to plan."

Hayley had to wonder what Charlotte's plans were for the day. But she was stopped from her thoughts as the receptionist told her how much her appointment had cost her.

"One hundred and forty pounds?! For a wash and trim?"

"Wash, blow-dry and cut. Plus all the products."

"Oh, sorry, I thought the shampoo and mousse would be in the price. Silly me."

"Well, if it helps, you look a lot better than when you arrived, miss."

"I guess, thank you, I think." Hayley gave her card over and hoped Tom wouldn't look at the bank statement this month. Not that he ever did.

But actually, he was thrilled when he saw her and said it was about time that she did something with her hair, however much it cost. So, in the end, she didn't know whether to be flattered or not.

But three days later, she stood in front of the mirror in her bedroom and knew that Tom was right. She had found a cream silk flower that she'd had in a vase for years to put in her hair, and after a quick rinse under the tap, it had come up as good as new.

Tom stood next to her in his old suit, but a new shirt and tie. They held hands and smiled as they looked at their reflections, seeing not two but three members of the family. They looked perfect to attend the society wedding of the year.

Chapter 15

So far, so good, thought Abigail. The bells of St Barnabas Church in Micklebrook were ringing like they did when she was a young girl and going to Sunday school. If she could still cry, she would have had a tear in her eye when she saw Hayley and Tom walk into the church arm in arm. They sat near the back on the left side after they had been shown to their seats by a handsome usher.

Suzie sat between Hayley and a lady who was wearing a huge hat on top of permed hair. She had strict instructions not to leave Hayley's side for the whole day. If there was going to be a murder, it wouldn't be their friend.

The other spirits—Abigail, Terry, Betty, and Lillian—were standing to one side, waiting for the bridesmaids and bride to arrive. Danny and his best man, Monty, were sitting on the front pew to the right. When the bells stopped ringing, signalling that the wedding party had entered the vestibule, the two men began to look a bit nervous and got to their feet. The excitement built as an elderly man started to play the organ when Charlotte and the maid of honour, Donna, walked down the aisle, followed by the girls, Eve and Ava.

There were gasps and smiles all round when the guests saw Amelia on the arm of Colonel Newberry. The only person who didn't look enthralled was Charlotte. If Abigail hadn't heard the bad things about the groom, she would have thought that Danny was genuinely in love with his bride. His face changed to pure joy when he saw her. Perhaps there was hope for them, and marriage would make the difference for him. But was he in love, or just a good actor? But even he could see how wonderful Amelia looked, and it wasn't just because her dress had cost over two thousand pounds. It had a strapless white bodice and a full tulle skirt, and there must have been thousands of crystal beads sewn on. For the church, the bride was wearing a white lace bolero, for reverence and warmth. A tiara finished off the princess effect, and Hayley noticed she was wearing her sister's bracelet as her 'borrowed'.

Abigail and her friends walked unseen around the 17th-century church like bodyguards protecting VIPs. Unseen only by the living, but watched suspiciously by a motley assortment of other ghosts from centuries past.

The first hymn and the readings happened without incident, and the vows sounded beautiful, even though they did sound as if they had been downloaded from Google. The only moment Hayley held her breath was when the vicar said, "If there is anyone present who knows of any lawful impediment to this marriage, then they should declare it now." She expected to hear a gunshot ring out in the silence, but all was quiet.

Abigail said, "Thank God for that."

It didn't seem long before the bride and groom could relax when they were pronounced husband and wife.

Although it was only March, the sun shone and the rain stayed away as the couple left through the arched door to have confetti thrown over them, and Philip Gowdy Photography was there to get the perfect shot. But everyone soon felt the chill while the other photographs were being taken, which seemed to go on for a long time. When the bridesmaids said they couldn't feel their arms anymore, they got in the first limousine, and Danny and Amelia left in the white one. The rest of the guests went up the lane for the five-minute walk to Micklebrook Priory.

"Well, that was a bit of an anticlimax," said Abigail. "The only shocking thing was that Danny's middle name is Reginald. I was sure the killer would want to make a statement at the ceremony."

"We'd know who it was then, dear. Unless they had planted a bomb earlier or something. Or put poison on the pen they signed the register with. Or put a deadly spider in Amelia's dress."

"True, but unlikely, Betty."

"So what happens at these posh weddings, then?" asked Lillian.

"You're asking the wrong people," said Terry. "Posh to me was a buffet at the Cock and Bottle."

Betty said, "I've been to some grand affairs. My own daughter had a lovely wedding at a country house. I even wore a hat. Usually, they start with drinks on trays and nibbles. Then they go in for the meal. You have to sit where they say, though. So you eat, have speeches and toasts, and then a disco and dancing."

"They're having a disco and a band. I hope they play some songs from the sixties," said Terry. "I'll show you how to do the rock 'n' roll, Abigail."

"You can try. I told you what happened when I took that line dancing class, didn't I? I don't suppose death has helped my two left feet."

"I can do the jitterbug, Terry," said Betty. "You couldn't get us off the floor once we started."

"That sounds like your John. At least someone will join me. I'll have to save the slow ones for Abigail. And the last one," he said with a wink.

Drinks on trays and nibbles didn't seem a fitting description of what actually came next. As the guests arrived, May Palmer showed them into a large marquee where they were served a choice of Pimm's, Buck's Fizz, or white wine and appetisers, while a string quartet played Bach and Mozart.

Hayley and Tom stood on their own for a while, Tom on Pimms and Hayley with a Buck's Fizz. Suzie called over to Abigail when Amelia joined them for a chat.

"Thank you so much for coming. I feel so much better knowing you're here. A psychic and a policeman can make you feel far safer," she said pleasantly.

"It's a beautiful wedding, Amelia. The music is perfect. And you look absolutely stunning."

"Thank you. I keep looking around, but I can't see anyone I don't know."

"We've been looking too," said Tom. "Hopefully, there won't be any trouble today. Could be that the attacker has already made his or her point, and it was nothing to do with you and Danny."

"Do you really think so, Tom?" Amelia sounded so relieved.

But Hayley didn't feel quite so sure all of a sudden, as a shiver ran through her body, but she said, "It will be fine, I'm sure."

"Thank goodness for that. So make sure you enjoy yourselves. We've put you with a few people you might know—some friends your age and my aunt and uncle. You'll see the table plan over there. It will give you the number of the table, and the names will be on it. May is over there if you can't find it. She's been amazing so far. She's been here since the crack of dawn, putting all the favours out and keeping on top of things. And she runs the whole thing like clockwork. Everything is timed to perfection. Well worth the money."

"Is she staying all day?"

"Just till we cut the cake later. Once the evening part starts, she'll go. Oh, did you see the cake? That Chris did a lovely job. How he makes those flowers, I'll never know."

"He made a lovely one for me. I picked it up yesterday from his house. Did you collect it from there?" asked Hayley.

"Goodness, no. He set it up this morning. He came about twelve, I think. I must remember to thank him. I hope it tastes as good as it looks. Anyway, I must find my gorgeous husband and mingle before we go in and eat. I couldn't face any breakfast, and I'm starving. Although I can't eat much with all the boning in this dress."

"It's well worth it looking at you. Where are we having the meal?"

"We hired the Great Hall. It's spectacular. The artwork and structures are fabulous. Do have another drink," said Amelia as a tray of drinks was brought to them.

"I'd better not, hun. I'm just allowing myself one for the toast. They say it's bad luck if you don't."

"Well, we don't want any of that. We'll catch up later. Where has my husband disappeared to?"

Lillian looked wistful as Amelia walked away. "I'd love to wear a dress like that. I never will now. I'm stuck in this nurse's uniform for eternity."

Abigail added, "It could be worse. You could be in pyjamas."

Terry said, "You're beautiful whatever you wear, love."

"And, Lillian, we'll never have to do our husbands' cooking and cleaning."

"You'd have done mine, wouldn't you, Abi?"

"Sorry, Terry. It's called equal rights, or women's lib."

"Or do it yourself," said Lillian.

Hayley was trying to listen to them, but she heard an announcement. May Palmer told everyone it was time to take their places in the Great Hall.

Chapter 16

HAYLEY AND TOM EVENTUALLY FOUND THEIR TABLE, which was right at the back of the room. Hayley wasn't too pleased to find that her table was number fourteen. The number thirteen had been missed she had noted, so essentially, she was on table thirteen, she reasoned. She hoped that wasn't another omen, but at that point, she wouldn't have been surprised if a crow had flown into the window. Something was in the air, and she remembered how she had told Amelia that if it was in the stars, there would be nothing she could do to stop it.

All the tables were round, apart from the one where Daniel and Amelia were sitting in the centre, with their families, bridesmaids, and best man on either side. As Danny had said, it was an assortment of families past and present.

At least Tom and she were facing the front. Some, like Auntie Pru and Uncle Robert, had their backs to everyone. Suzie stood behind Hayley to guard her but looked with envy at a small group of children who were playing in the corner of the room. She was too young to have envisaged herself as a bride, but she would have loved to be one of the bridesmaids and have a pretty dress on, like a princess.

Hayley couldn't drink, but she made sure she ate as much as she could of the exquisite food. The starter was Wild Salmon Terrine, and although Hayley had always said she would never eat duck, she managed to clear that plate as well. And when Tom said he didn't think he could eat his Eton Mess Cheesecake, she ate that too. "It would be rude to leave it on the plate," she told him.

Hayley could hardly move, but there was a gap between the meal and the speeches, so, like everyone else, she went to use the facilities.

"Are you going to the loo, Hayley?" shouted Abigail from the other side of the room. She forgot for a moment that all the guests couldn't hear her. Hayley rolled her eyes and nodded.

"Good, we'll come with you."

"Oh, good," said Hayley through gritted teeth. "Have you seen anything suspicious?" she whispered as they stood in the queue.

"We thought that May looked a bit dodgy while you were all eating, so we followed her. But she only went outside to have an e-cigarette. Charlotte doesn't look too happy, and she's been knocking back the red wine. It could kick off with Amelia later. But I think it will be more that she's getting mouthy. She might even pass out before then, with a bit of luck."

"Amelia said Chris was here earlier with the cake; he may still be. I haven't even looked at the waiters—he could be one of them. Watch out for William Murphy too," Hayley told her.

"It's very hard to hear what you're saying with your hand over your mouth, you know."

Hayley shook her head and went into the cubicle, almost expecting them to follow her. But five minutes later, followed closely by Suzie, she went back to sit next to Tom, who was talking to Auntie Pru and Uncle Robert about the joys and perils of owning a cat.

"Where is everyone? They'd better hurry up," said Hayley.

The Templetons and Newberrys had made their way back to the top table, and at last, the others, but Amelia and Danny were still missing. Hayley heard someone say that they had gone up to the bridal suite to freshen up. May was about to go and fetch them, as they were now three minutes behind schedule, when they entered to spontaneous applause.

May tapped a glass carefully with a knife and said, "Pray be silent for the father of the bride, Colonel Henry."

"Ladies and gentlemen, I'll start by thanking you all for coming to celebrate the marriage of Amelia and Daniel. It's lovely to see everyone here today, and I'd like to welcome his family to ours. And can I say how beautiful my daughter looks, and I have never felt so proud as I did when I walked her down the aisle.

Now that they have tied the knot, the key is communication —something that my lovely wife and I took some time to perfect. It was proven as soon as we returned from our honeymoon when I told her I liked black underwear. After which, she stopped washing my pants.

I knew right from the beginning that Amelia would be special, and she is. She's caring, thoughtful, loving, and beautiful. And some would say that in her father's eyes, she can do no wrong. And I know Daniel will treat her right; I feel it in my gun —I mean my gut.

So let us raise our glasses for the toast and make a wish. In the words of the fairytale—to Amelia and Daniel, may you live happily ever after."

Hayley noticed that the only person who hadn't enjoyed the speech was Charlotte. Although she looked at Daniel when his father-in-law had mentioned his gun, and he was the only person who hadn't seen the funny side of the joke. Hayley joined the others in picking up her champagne flute, which had now been filled, and said, "To the bride and groom."

The colonel took his seat as May tapped the glass again. "And now we'll hear from the—"

But the only thing that was heard was a guttural groan from someone and a scream from the top table. Tom heard a gasp and went into police mode. Hayley ran after him, but she couldn't see what had happened, as everyone was on their feet. But as Tom moved them back, while telling them he was a policeman, she saw what she was dreading. One of the party was face down, with her chin resting on the white tablecloth, the stem of a champagne flute gripped in her hand. Her eyes stared ahead, and her mouth was open. Tom called out for a doctor, but one was not needed to know that this person was dead.

Chapter 17

DANIEL WAS SHAKING HIS MOTHER AND TELLING HER to breathe, but Fiona never would again, so Tom pulled him gently away to a chair further down the table. Then he nodded to Hayley to comfort him. Everyone else was staring in shock, so Tom tried to move them without pushing too much. But no one could take their eyes off the mother of the groom, dead, on what should have been one of the happiest days of her life.

"I'm Police Constable Tom Bennett from Gorebridge Police. Could you all move away, please, and not touch anything until we know exactly what's happened? Has anyone got their phone on them? Please could you ring 999, sir," he said to the best man, Monty. In a louder voice, he said to the room, "Just as a precaution, can you make sure that no one leaves the venue? We'll need some information from you first."

The photographer had started to take photographs, and Tom shouted at him to stop immediately. "I'll take that off you if you take any more." That made Philip move quickly away. He wasn't going to lose all the pictures of the day. They could be worth a fortune after this.

May, the wedding planner, had turned pale but asked Tom if there was anything that she could do.

"Could you take everyone that wasn't on this table into the marquee? Let them have a drink or something."

"Of course. The band is just setting up in there, but I don't suppose they'll be needed now. How dreadful for the family. Do you know what happened to her?"

"I wouldn't like to say. But I need to do my job. You'll have a list of all the guests, won't you? When you get the chance, my boss will need a copy."

"I've got one with me to check the seating plan, in case there were some no-shows. I'll settle the others and find it."

"Is there a room where the family could go?" He then whispered, "In case this is a crime scene."

"Oh, God. I thought it was. They could wait in the orangery. Poisoning?"

"Too early to say. But please keep it to yourself."

Abigail couldn't listen to any more. "Of course it's a poisoning. We knew it, didn't we, Terry? We should never have called it a date. Something always happens."

"It's like a curse. But why her? Her name's Fiona, isn't it?"

"Yes. That's what we've got to find out. It could be random. Anyone at the top table could have been targeted. Suzie, don't you leave Hayley alone for one second."

"I haven't, and I won't."

Hayley left Danny to the care of Amelia, who was as upset as he was. Whether it was the loss of her mother-in-law or her wedding day, she wasn't sure. But she saw Amelia look accusingly at her, as if it was somehow her fault. She felt guilty enough because she hadn't been able to stop what she had predicted. Hayley shook her head in acknowledgement and then noticed that Charlotte's bracelet wasn't the only thing that was borrowed. Amelia must have decided to wear the pearl earrings—loaned to her by Fiona.

"You were right, Abigail," Hayley whispered.

"I know. But about what in particular?"

"Something borrowed. Amelia is wearing Danny's mum's earrings. I wonder who knew beforehand that she was. That could have been why Fiona was chosen. And she's wearing her sister's bracelet."

"I often wish I was wrong," Abigail said modestly. "Lillian, could you watch Charlotte? We don't want a dead bridesmaid. It's not a very good advert for our detective agency."

"Surely I'd be better here, looking at the body."

"Sorry, you're right."

"I'll do it," said Terry. "Just keep me in the loop. And if you hear me shout, come running."

"Thanks, darling," she said as she kissed him on the cheek. Terry followed the mourners to the orangery, while wondering what that even was—only to find out that it was a fancy conservatory.

"So, Lillian, what do you reckon?" asked Abigail.

"Poisoned, more than likely. See the slight frothing around the lips? At least she went fast. It must have been in the champagne for the toast."

"I think so too. It could have been given earlier, but the chances of her dying after one sip would be too much."

Tom was talking to Mills on his mobile, and Hayley mouthed that she needed to talk to him, so he finished the call. "Tom, those glasses have been there since this morning with place cards, so the poison could have been put there any time. And Chris Jenkins delivered the cake. But it could have been after the meal. Everyone was moving about, so it could be anyone. You were here then. Did you see anyone up here?"

"I was talking, so I didn't notice. Johnson will have a field day. A waitress—or was it a waiter?—filled the champagne flutes, and I can't even say who did our table, let alone pick one out of a lineup for this table. We'll need a list of the waiting staff as well."

Betty said to Lillian and Abigail, "I can't think that anyone meant to kill her myself. Her poor husband was shaking like a leaf. At least his daughters are here. They'll look after him. What's the saying? Um, a daughter's a wife till a son has a life."

"I don't think I've heard that one," said Lillian.

"I'm not sure that's it. A daughter's a life till you have a wife. No, a wife's a life ..."

Hayley surprised Tom by suddenly snapping, "A daughter's a daughter all of your life; a son's a son till he takes a wife."

"Thank you, dear. But you don't have to shout."

"I'm sorry, Betty. But I feel so ashamed that I couldn't do anything to stop this poor woman from being killed. Like if I hadn't said that all those years ago, nothing would have happened."

Tom and the others all told her that it wasn't her fault.

"Why do I feel so guilty then? Abigail, if you never solve a murder again, you must solve this."

"Er, excuse me, I am the real investigator here."

"I'm sorry, Tom. We'll do it together."

He answered, "Let's have a look at the names before Johnson gets here. So, on the end, we have Donna, the maid of honour. Monty, the best man. Tim—who's that?"

"Danny's real dad. Then Susan, his stepmum. George, his stepdad."

They walked behind Fiona's body.

"Danny next to her. Then Amelia, the colonel, and Harriet. And next to her, Charlotte and then Daniel's stepsisters. I think we can discount them. They're far too young."

"Are you saying it could be any of the others?" asked Tom.

"The two sets of parents wouldn't have wanted their day to end like this. I hadn't even thought of the best man. I wonder if he had a thing for Amelia."

"Not the way he was all over Charlotte," said Abigail. "And then there's all the suspects we had before—Chris, that William Murphy, Saloni's husband, Darren. Or someone we don't even know about."

"If you're trying to cheer me up, it's not working, hun. I think we can discount Danny now, don't you?"

"Definitely not. For all we know, he needs money fast, and now he's inheriting it. Or maybe she was about to change her will and leave it to her husband. I know you always see the best in people, Hayley, but I think it always pays to think the worst."

"It happens," said Betty. "It could even be that May woman. Could be a case of always the planner, never the bride."

"Very true," said Hayley, then went back to talking to Tom. "I can hear sirens, can you? I wonder what mood the inspector will be in today. Hopefully, his good lady hasn't come to her senses."

Luckily, Detective Chief Inspector Johnson was still full of the joys of spring.

"So, you've put a curse on some poor couple's wedding now, have you, Mrs Bennett?" But at least he said it pleasantly.

"Nothing to do with me. I don't actually do curses, but I suppose I could start," she said, looking deep into his eyes.

"No offence, love. Just my little jest. Well, it looks like a lovely wedding. I wonder how much something like this would set you back."

"About ten thousand, probably. Are you thinking of one yourself?" asked Hayley.

"Me? You never know. Right, who's the one that spoiled my Saturday?"

"This is the mother of the groom." Tom had to look at the place card. "Fiona, Daniel Templeton's mother. Fiona Arnold, actually; she had remarried. Colonel Newberry had given his speech and made a toast to the couple, and we all took a sip, and she went face first. The doctor hasn't come yet, but I checked, and she had no pulse."

"Good lad. I wonder what the poison was. Can't smell any almonds. Could be anything. Could be a powder or something like liquid strychnine. Toxicology test will tell us. We'll need to do a good search. They would have had to have a method of storing it. Unless it was a pill. So, who could have done it?"

"Anyone. The glasses have been here way before the reception started. I'll have to check with the kitchen at what time. And after the meal, everyone was walking about. And the glasses were filled by the staff for the toast."

"Good, here's Mills. Dave, you come with me, and we'll talk to her relations. Tom, you stay here and wait for the doctor and the forensic team. Where is the not-so-happy couple?"

"In the orangery, sir. Through that door and to the right. All the other guests are in the marquee."

"Orangery? Marquee and Great Hall? Can't these people call anything like normal folk? Mills, get the uniforms to watch the guests. Take their details and ask if they saw anything, and then they can go. I suppose they won't get to cut the cake now. What a waste. Hey, didn't we have a cakemaker killed the other day?"

"Yes, sir," said Mills. "And a dressmaker and a florist."

Hayley took a chance because Johnson seemed in such a good mood.

"Tony, I know someone who thinks it might have something to do with the saying—something old, something new, something borrowed, something blue. It's for luck."

"What a load of cobblers. Didn't get much luck today, did they? But it'll be a sorry day when we need one of your airy-fairy friends telling us our jobs."

Hayley bristled. "I didn't mean it like that. I'm saying the killer is using it as a motive. It's a clue. Listen, something old—the antique knife that was used to kill Saloni Kaye. The 'new', scissors that killed Miriam Bell. Something blue is the ribbon around Mrs Merry's neck, and I happen to know that Amelia borrowed Fiona's earrings."

"As I said, what a load of cobblers. What's she even doing here, Bennett? What do you reckon, Mills?"

"Seems to fit, sir. At least someone's making it fit. Perhaps as a red herring."

"Red herring? You've been reading too much Agatha Christie, lad. But if you're right, it doesn't help us to know who it is, does it? When you know whodunit, Mrs Bennett, come back. Till then, you'd better get out. It's a crime scene, so you shouldn't be in here. Where were you sitting?"

"At the back, on table fourteen."

"Bit of an afterthought, were you? Okay, off you go, love, and leave the police work to the police. If I need someone to read a crystal ball, I'll be in touch. Huh, something old, something new —honestly, give me strength. Something murdered more like."

Chapter 18

HAYLEY RELUCTANTLY LEFT THE GREAT HALL AND made her way to the marquee with Suzie by her side. The other ghosts went to see what Johnson would say to the poor husband and son.

The only people Hayley could see whom she felt she could talk to were Auntie Pru and Uncle Robert. Hayley had never felt so much sadness and despair in one place. In one corner, the four-tiered cake stood high on a stand, a monument to what should have been.

Auntie Pru waved her over. "Is she really dead?"

"I'm afraid so. The CID is there now. They don't know what happened yet. Did you know Fiona well?"

"I met her a couple of times. The last time was for Harriet's fiftieth at the Winston. That was a lovely do."

Hayley had a thought. "Did she have a cake?"

"Yes, a beautiful one. Funnily enough, Harriet told me that the one who baked it had been killed as well. What is going on? I feel so sorry for Daniel. How will he ever get over his mother dying on his wedding day?"

"If it is murder, it will be even worse. But we don't know yet. She might have been ill."

"I can't believe it's murder, Hayley. Things like that don't happen in the Chiltern Hills. It's not like living in a big city. Everyone knows everyone here."

"You'd be surprised, Prudence. Knowing someone and their secrets can produce some very good motives for murder. Say someone had put something in her drink—did you see anyone go near her glass? Or did you leave after the meal, like me?"

"No, I was there the whole time. But don't forget, my back was to it. There were plenty of people walking past, but I didn't take much notice. So I'm not a very good witness."

Uncle Robert said, "Nor me. I went outside for a puff."

"So, Prudence, did you see who filled up the glasses for the toast?"

"I did on our table—a nice young man. I remarked how well he was doing to not spill a drop, and he said a drop was probably worth more than his shoes cost."

"Could you describe him?"

"About thirty or under. Brown hair—short at the sides like they all have it now. He had the white shirt and black waistcoat and bow tie like all the others. He had a nice face, so I could definitely pick him out of a lineup."

"It probably won't come to that. I'm wondering if someone wearing the same would have been noticed."

"Ooh, they could have put on a beard and glasses. It would be easier for a man rather than a woman. How many men here are wearing black three-piece suits? They would only have to take off their jacket and put on an elastic bow tie."

"You're good at this, Prudence."

"Murder, She Wrote," she laughed. "I've seen them all, haven't I, Robert? I've even got some of the books. I wish I'd turned around—I could have been a witness. I might be able to think of something else. I have a feeling that I did see something extraordinary today, but I can't for the life of me remember what."

Hayley took a chance on her fellow sleuth. "You may not know this, but I'm a psychic medium, and I've helped the police a few times."

"I thought I recognised you. Are you Hayley Moon, not Bennett?"

"I use that when I'm working."

"How exciting. It's like that programme about a medium who has three little girls and solves crime. What was that called now?"

"Er, Medium?"

"That's it. I loved that. So you do the same?"

"Not really. The police aren't quite so grateful for my help, unfortunately. They think it's more of a hindrance. But that's never stopped me. Anyway, I have a few friends, and we run an agency to help anyone with problems—not always murder. Can I give you my card and you ring me if you think of anything else?"

"Could you hypnotise me so I remember, like in that other one I watch?"

"I don't think so. But when you get the chance, sit in your armchair and close your eyes. Empty your head, and it might appear. A smell or a colour might bring it back to you."

"Like the flowers on the table? Or the wine?"

"Exactly. Sometimes it just pops back there."

Prudence looked at the card.

The Deadly Detective Agency
All Problems Great & Small
Paranormal & Normal

Followed by an email address and mobile number for Hayley Moon.

"Are you kept busy?"

"It's been a bit slow this year, but at the moment, we're working on a few cases—ones connected to this and another one concerning a mysterious painting, but that will have to wait. We don't make much money. In fact, if we do, we donate it to a lady who lost her daughter, Suzie, to a hit and run." Hayley didn't think she could add that Suzie was standing right next to her.

"Amazing. I'm so glad we talked, Hayley. I felt dreadful, but now I've got something to focus on. We were so looking forward to today. It's not often we have a weekend away. I don't suppose we'll be able to stay now. I spent a fortune on my outfit and fascinator. Oh no, I've just thought—I left it on the table! They won't throw it away, will they?"

"I'm sure they won't. I tell you what—I can see May, the planner, over there; I'll ask her. I reckon she'll be here after us, so Tom might let her grab it. I better not—I'm in enough trouble with his DCI."

Hayley left them and went to ask May if she could have a word. "Can I ask you a favour?"

"You were with the policeman, weren't you? Do you know what's going to happen? Everyone is asking me when they can go."

"The uniforms will be going round to talk to everyone first to get details, and then the guests can leave. Amelia's Auntie Pru has left her fascinator on table fourteen; could you grab it for her if you get the chance?"

"I don't see why not. I've got to speak to the inspector, so I'll ask. There's not much I can tell them about Fiona, though."

"I think he'll want to know who could have had access to her glass if it is a suspicious death. What time were the glasses put on the table, do you know?"

"Of course, I know everything; that's my job. The service began at three, so I told them to lay the table at eleven. You can't do it too early if you want it to look fresh. The three glasses go on last—water, wine, and flutes. Not quite last, actually. I put the name cards in place. Amelia and her mother had told me where everyone had to sit. The only trouble with that was that when Amelia came to look at the room, she realised that there were thirteen on the top table. She went mad, but it was too late to do anything about it. The seating plan had been printed by then. It was hard enough to place everyone with all the stepparents. The colonel's ex-wife has got three daughters who she wanted to be flower girls, but in the end, none of them were invited."

"They say thirteen for dinner is bad luck. And I noticed there was no thirteenth table."

"That was Amelia as well. She'd got it in her head that something was going to happen. She must be very superstitious. I've no idea why."

"Nor me," said Hayley, rather guiltily. "Mind you, she was right, wasn't she? Unlucky for some, thirteen. And I've just remembered that the roses on the tables were red and white. Isn't there a saying 'blood and bandages'?"

"Oh, don't you start. There are loads of superstitions. You can't take notice of all of them. Amelia just wanted red and white because it matched the decor in the room."

"Yes, you're right, sorry. I wonder what will happen to the cake now. What time did the cake arrive?"

"About noon. It was Chris, from Cakealicious. I told him where to put it and left him to it. I didn't see him leave."

"Who did the flowers?"

"Mrs Merry from Becklesfield. But she's in hospital, so the young girl that works for her brought them with her boyfriend. She did a lovely job. She put the displays on the tables, and I took the bouquets up to the bridal suite."

"Can you think of anyone who would want to spoil the day like this?"

"And the other times in the last couple of weeks?" said May. "I'm not stupid, you know. I think if anyone wanted to spoil the day, it would be as payback to Daniel. I can't take to him. Call it women's intuition. I've known him for a while. He was the best man for a wedding I did a few years ago, and he offered to do some marketing for me—advertising on all the social media platforms. I paid him upfront, but he never did finish what I paid him for. I wouldn't trust him further than I could throw him."

"It must have been a shock when you saw each other again. Did he say anything?"

"Not about work. He made out it was because of him that they were using me. I don't think he felt any embarrassment at all. But I feel for him today. No one deserves to see their mother die."

"As you say, it could well be payback. Between us, do you think it could be an old girlfriend?"

"Between us, I think it could be a present girlfriend."

Hayley excused herself as she had seen Jane Nichols and three other police constables enter the marquee. She went to talk to them, and they agreed that she could go. It had some perks being pregnant and married to a policeman.

Chapter 19

LILLIAN AND BETTY WERE FOLLOWING DAVE MILLS, and Abigail and Terry were staying close to Johnson. He'd already upset the colonel and his wife by saying they wouldn't be talked to first. He said they would have to wait their turn and told Dave that he wanted to talk to the husband first.

"What do I say, Sergeant? It's always the husband."

But it never is, thought Mills. He went and got George and asked him to come with him. The orangery was large enough that they could use a table in the far corner without being overheard. Mills joined his boss and sat opposite the red-eyed husband of Fiona.

"Sit down, sir. I'm Detective Chief Inspector Johnson, and this is Sergeant Mills. So your name is George Templeton?"

"George Arnold. I'm Daniel's stepfather. I married his mother, Fiona, three years ago after my wife died."

"I see. Well, I'm sorry for your loss. Do you know if your wife suffered from seizures at all?"

"Oh God, is that what that was? As far as I knew, she didn't. Mind you, she did suffer from headaches sometimes."

"Most wives do, sir. Especially at night, as I remember."

"I don't think this is the time to joke, Inspector."

"It's either a seizure, or she was poisoned then," Johnson snapped. "But we won't know for sure until tomorrow, after the postmortem. Did she have any enemies or anyone that had something against her?"

"Not enough to kill her. She was a sweet person inside and out. We're just normal churchgoing people."

"In my experience, that doesn't make you free from sin or any more popular."

"Could it be an accident? Bleach in the glass, perhaps?"

"Unlikely, but we will check for natural causes. Any allergies?"

"No."

"Where were you after the meal, before the speeches?"

"I walked around with Fiona for a while. We talked to my children—those two over there. They'd gone to the marquee to talk to their friends. They weren't very happy that they had to sit with us and not their friends for the meal. Then I went outside for an e-cigarette. I smoked for years, and now I'm addicted to them. Fiona went to the ladies, and she was already back in her seat when I got back. And that was the last time I will ever speak to her," said George as his voice broke.

"Like I said, we are very sorry, sir. You can go and sit down again. Someone will need to officially identify the body, but not till tomorrow. Thank you. Mills, go and get the son."

"I'm DCI Johnson, and this is Sergeant Mills. Could you give me your name and your relationship to the deceased, please?"

"Daniel Templeton, and she's my mother. It's my wedding."

"Yes, I'm sorry, sir. It must be hard for you. Had your mother been ill recently or had fits before?"

"No. She always said how she hadn't been to the doctor's for years. She was proud of that. Someone did it to her, didn't they? I'll kill them when I find out who."

"We don't advise that, sir. And we don't know what

happened yet. Let us do our jobs, please. Did you see anyone go near her glass or act suspiciously?"

"I would have told you."

"What did you do just before your father-in-law's speech?"

"Er, I can't think now. Um, I went to the bridal suite with Amelia. She wanted to retouch her lipstick and that. You know, that kind of thing."

"I don't, but I can imagine, sir. That's all, then. You'll all need to give statements at the station tomorrow."

"Can we go to our rooms yet?"

"Not till they've been searched, I'm afraid. Your wedding night will have to wait."

"I can assure you that is the furthest thing from my mind. I think we'll just go home. But it's up to Amelia, I suppose."

"Yes, sir. You're married now. You've made your last decisions," laughed Johnson.

Daniel rolled his eyes but also had a slight smile on his face. He agreed with that.

The colonel stormed over with a frown on his face. His downturned moustache made him look even angrier.

"Will this take much longer? My wife and I want to go to our room."

"What you'd like makes no bones to me, sir. Who are you anyway? Let me guess—Colonel Newberry."

"Yes. And I know Chief Constable Carson. He and I are very good friends."

"I'll be sure to say hello for you. We have others to see before you. Now go and sit down, please. Unless you'd like to talk down at the station."

The colonel turned red with anger and went back to the others.

"He didn't take that well, sir. Are you sure that was wise?" said Mills.

"Don't care, son. He looked like he was going to explode,

didn't he? He's not going to be pleased that we have to search the rooms. Make sure you speak to the bride next."

"Where are you going?"

"Sergeant, I've got a very important date with a lovely lady," said Johnson with a smile like Mills had never seen before. "I have great faith in you, and I'll see you in the morning." And off he went.

Chapter 20

HAYLEY AND SUZIE WENT HOME IN TOM'S CAR. SHE knew he would be working late and get a lift from one of the others. The other members of the agency stayed at the venue, and they didn't meet till the next morning.

Tom had gone in early and left Hayley and Luna in bed. The lazy cat had been fed and ran straight up to snuggle down with Hayley, even though all through the night he was next to Tom. The King is dead, long live the Queen, Tom thought. He knew that would change as soon as he got home again. He hadn't even wanted the scraggly-looking, half-dead kitten when Hayley had brought him home. But within days, Luna had chosen his favourite, and Tom loved him to death.

Abigail and the others reluctantly let Hayley have a lie-in. It was Sunday, after all. They waited patiently downstairs until she joined them at eleven. And that was only because Luna had been meowing for early lunch.

As they talked, they all felt depressed, and Hayley wasn't the only one to feel guilty. They could only imagine how bad everyone felt in the Newberry and Templeton households. This was the first murder that was so close to home for Hayley, and she couldn't get up the enthusiasm for sleuthing. Even the word sleuthing seemed disrespectful. But they owed it to Amelia to find out the truth, or else Hayley would always be guilty in her eyes. This murder didn't just affect one family; there were two hundred guests at the wedding who had all seen a woman die before their very eyes. As much as she would have liked to leave it to the police, Hayley forced herself to talk about it.

"Tom said they didn't find much out after we left. They didn't find a bottle of poison or anything. The postmortem is today, but I think we all know what it will show."

"I'm surprised her spirit isn't still here," said Betty. "That must be the quickest death ever. I suppose she might still be there somewhere."

Terry nodded. "I think Betty and I should go back to Micklebrook. She might be at the Priory or at the church. I don't think she'll have any idea who killed her, but we could help her."

"Agreed," said Abigail. "Hayley, you should stay here and rest with Lillian and Suzie."

"Hold your knickers a minute. Just because I'm pregnant doesn't mean I can't help. My body might be slightly bigger. Yes, slightly, Abigail, but my brain still works."

"I meant because it's Sunday, actually, and everywhere is shut."

"Yeah, right, sorry. I was thinking that I could get Lady Caroline to help me if I go to see anyone." Lady Caroline Hatton was the owner of Chiltern Hall and often helped with their cases. She was one of only a few who knew that a detective agency was being run from the other side.

"As long as Suzie goes too. Who were you thinking of paying a visit to?"

"I'm not sure. I think May is hiding something. And don't forget Caroline used to be a theatrical actress in London. I'm thinking that Miss, er, Agatha Fletcher is getting married in September. And her husband..."

"Hercule?" said Betty.

"A bit obvious. And her husband, Arthur Hastings, needs a wedding planner."

"Maybe Caroline could pay her condolences to the colonel and family then. I bet she knows them. They're quite high up in the county hierarchy," said Abigail.

"I'll give her a ring now." As Hayley walked out of the room, they heard her say, "Morning, Caroline. How do you fancy getting the greasepaint out and doing a bit of undercover work?"

Lillian asked, "What else should we do?"

Abigail thought for a minute. "I wonder if there's any way we could get to look at the photographs that were taken yesterday. Every time I saw him—Philip, I think it was—he was snapping away. I wonder if Johnson has thought of it. Hayley can tell Tom, but I'd like to see them first."

"We might even be in some of them, dear. It wouldn't be the first time. I'm thinking Agatha Fletcher might need a photographer. Hayley could go with her. We need to go quickly before the police take them. Grab the bull by its horn, so to speak."

"Painful, if not dangerous, Betty. But yes, a good idea. Suzie could go through the photos then."

Hayley came back and felt a lot happier now that she had something she could do.

"Caroline does know the Newberrys, so she'll go and see them when she feels the time is right. And she said she'd love to go for an appointment at May's Days. Although from now on, it should be May Day, May Day."

"Yes. SOS. We couldn't save Fiona's day," said Abigail sadly.

Betty asked, "Is Caroline looking forward to going ignocnoti, ignoto, ignotogo?"

"She is looking forward to going ig, ingot, undercover, Betty. Hopefully, we'll get an appointment for tomorrow."

"Oh, and Agatha Fletcher will need a photographer as well,"

said Abigail. "We have to go and have a look at yesterday's pics, Hayley. We might see someone doing something they shouldn't."

"Great idea. Or see someone who shouldn't be there, like William Murphy or Chris, hun."

"Or anyone, actually," said Abigail. "We mustn't forget Saloni's husband."

"Darren Kaye? He's got an alibi, dear, for his wife's murder."

"He could have killed his wife before. I've just had a brilliant idea."

"Aren't all your ideas brilliant, Abigail?" said Terry, tongue firmly in cheek.

"Nice of you to say, but this one is particularly brilliant. Listen, Saloni was in the kitchen baking. Lillian, could he have killed her earlier, but made the body temperature higher by leaving the cooker on? He could have had it on full and then turned it down. We'll have to ask Tom if the oven was on. They might not have thought anything about it."

"Yes, it would have made the body temperature higher, so she could have died before they thought."

"And Darren might have had a partner or a girlfriend that helped. Didn't Mills tell Tom he had a rather good-looking receptionist that was his alibi? Once he was excluded from his wife's murder, they didn't look at him for the others. We need to look at those photos. If he, or she, was anywhere near that wedding, we've got them. You'll have to tell Tom tonight and get him to send you photos of them. We saw William, but not Darren Kaye," Abigail told her. Then she leaned back in deep thought. "What if he was the one that was making sure Chris lost customers so there was another suspect?"

"One way to find out," said Hayley as she turned on her phone. "Chris, sorry to ring you on a Sunday. Yes, I did hear. I was there. I wanted to say how pleased I was with the cake you made for the baby shower. No, I haven't tasted it yet, but it's perfect, so I want to give you a good review. I was wondering, do you know who it was that made you lose those customers? You have no idea. Okay, I'll be giving you five stars anyway. Thank you. Bye. Well, that's no help. But why would Kaye have wanted to kill his wife?"

Abigail said, "For all we know, she's the one with the money. He wanted to run off with his fancy bit, and he's got the wife insured. Tom will find out, I'm sure."

"But why kill the others?" asked Terry. "Seems a bit over the top to me."

"As a distraction. If he suddenly gets an insurance payout for a couple of million, even Johnson would think he's guilty. This way, it looks like a crazed serial killer with a thing for weddings. So tomorrow, Terry and Betty must go to find Fiona, and we'll go to see the photographer and find the proof."

"Well done, Abigail. Perhaps then we can get back to the painting. Every time I go in the kitchen and see it hanging there, I feel I should be doing something for her," Hayley reminded them.

"As soon as we've caught Darren Kaye, we'll go and see Celia Hanson. I bet she knows about the murder of someone called Pippa, even if it was a long time ago."

Chapter 21

UNFORTUNATELY, MAY'S DAYS DID NOT HAVE AN appointment for Agatha Fletcher until Tuesday, so no disguise was needed on the Monday. It was a shame because Lady Caroline Hatton was looking forward to donning a wig and greasepaint, but she decided she could use a professional photographer for the upcoming gymkhana and her other charity occasions, so she could go as herself.

Hayley arranged to meet her friend outside Philip Gowdy's studio in the busy street in Boxford, where she had a lot of trouble parking outside. Hayley had never got the hang of parallel parking. And trying not to bash the front of the chauffeur-driven Jaguar made it even more nerve-wracking. When she managed it after four attempts, Caroline got out.

"Don't laugh. I don't know if it's just me or all women, but I can't park. I know it's sexist, and if Terry said it, I'd be furious, but men seem to have the knack."

"I didn't say a word. I have no problem with parking—the chauffeur does it beautifully," Caroline laughed.

"And it doesn't help having Lillian and Abigail chattering in my ears. Telling me left or right, and 'you could get a bus in there.' Suzie's here as well, but she's an angel."

After Caroline had said hello to them, while looking in the wrong direction, they went into the little shop to meet Philip.

"Lady Hatton, please take a seat. I'm sorry, it's turned very chilly in here suddenly."

"Thank you. This is Hayley, a friend of mine."

"Hello. We actually met at the wedding on Saturday, Philip. I said how well you'd done, and I knew Caroline was looking for a photographer."

"Thank you. It didn't end well, though. I can't get the last photo I took out of my mind."

"Have you looked at the photos yet?"

"I took over eight hundred altogether. So far, I've only got up to the ones at the church."

Lady Caroline took the opportunity to ask, "Could I have a look at them, please, to give me an idea of your work? I organise a lot of charities, and social media is a large part of that now."

"I've got my portfolio here. You said on the phone you might need me for a gymkhana, so are you sure you wouldn't rather see the ones I've taken of horses? I'm featured in various magazines and done countless calendars. You could see how the ones of their movements come out."

"I won't be using you just for the gymkhana. But the ones from the wedding are the most recent ones. If you wouldn't mind."

"Of course. They're on my laptop. I'm sure the bride and groom won't mind. It'll give you an idea of my work."

Philip went round to their side and clicked on the file under the heading Newberry-Micklebrook. "I'd better go past the ones of Amelia getting ready in her room."

"Oh, you were at the Priory first, then?" Interesting, thought Hayley as Philip scrolled through until he got to the vows.

"I was. That's strange, though. On some of them, you can

almost see a ball of light. Look, there are four next to the altar. I noticed them on some of the others. I have no idea why."

"Orbs," said Hayley and frowned at Abigail and the others.

Lady Caroline said, "Beautiful photographs, I must say. May I?"

"Of course, please do," said Philip as he moved aside. "Those are as we went outside. I got a fantastic one of the confetti being thrown."

"I don't suppose I could have a cup of tea, could I?" Caroline asked, clearing her throat. "Milk, two sugars."

"Coffee, please, white with sugar," added Hayley, hoping it would take him longer.

"Of course. I'm sorry, I should have offered. I've got some biscuits somewhere."

Abigail spoke excitedly for the first time after he had gone. "Right, we've got three minutes at most. Get to the meal."

After one minute, they were still seeing people eating. The waiters who happened to be in the shots were unknown to them, and there was no sign of William Murphy, Chris, or Darren Kaye. Then they looked at snaps of random people as Philip walked around the room after the meal and some that were taken outside, where a group of smokers were standing, including Charlotte, May, and Uncle Robert. The top table was empty in most of them. The only suspicious one was of Charlotte and Daniel standing near it. Neither looked happy, and he must have lied when he said he went straight to the room with Amelia. In the next one, Daniel was walking away, and Charlotte looked furious.

"Wow, if looks could kill," said Abigail.

"He'd be dead," said Lillian.

Hayley added, "Perhaps Fiona was killed by mistake. She was right next to her son, Daniel. It's easy to pick something up from the wrong side. I ate Tom's roll before I realised. He thought I'd done it on purpose so I could eat both. More suspects, though—that's all we need. Tom will have to tell Dave to get a warrant to look at these."

Philip came back all too soon. "Here we are. Sorry, I've only got mugs."

"That's perfectly fine, thank you. Your photographs are excellent. We went through them all, and they suddenly stopped."

"The last one I took was the death of that poor lady."

"Let me see," said Lady Caroline. "What a terrible memory for you to keep. But it will be worth a fortune, I expect. I'm sure the tabloids would let you name your price."

"Do you think so? Oh no, I couldn't do that. But do you really think so?"

"I do. Well, the good news is that I'd like to book you for the gymkhana to start with. I'll get my assistant to email you the details. If you could then let me know your prices, I'm sure we'll come to an arrangement. Hopefully, no one will die."

"It's the first time it's happened, I can assure you."

"Have you any idea who could have done such a thing, Philip?"

"Hayley will have more of an idea than me. She's married to the police constable in that last photo."

"The police have no idea yet. Did you know any of them personally?"

"I'd met most of them. Amelia and Daniel both work, so it was easier to see them at home in the evenings. I went to Amelia's house, and both sets of parents were there. They were very nice. The colonel was... well, like you'd expect him to be. I would have thought he would have been the most likely victim. Sorry, I shouldn't say that."

Lady Caroline smiled at him. "Don't worry, I've met him and quite agree. Well, thank you very much for the tea, and you'll hear from me soon."

"Philip," said Hayley. "I really think you should let the police see these. You might have the photograph of the murderer who shouldn't be there. Imagine the publicity if you solved the case. The family would be very grateful as well. Ask for Sergeant Mills at the Gorebridge Police Station."

"You're right. Thank you. I'll make copies for them and ring them now."

They said their goodbyes and went outside, where Lady Caroline asked, "So what now, Hayley?"

"I looked up the address for Darren Kaye's business; it's called Anexis. It's not far from here. What do you think, Abigail?"

"I think we should see if Tom can look at the photos properly and see if he was at the wedding first. Mills knows what the receptionist looks like, and they can blow them up. And he can check if he had his wife insured for a lot of money."

Hayley told Caroline and said, "Terry and Betty are back at Micklebrook to see if they can see poor Fiona. She might be a lost soul somewhere."

"That's so sad. Is there anything I can do to help?" asked Caroline hopefully.

"We need another meeting," said Lillian, and Hayley passed this on to Caroline.

"We do," said Abigail thoughtfully. "It's like I've got all the pieces of a jigsaw in the right place, but it's not showing Darren Kaye. It's more like a Picasso, and I don't like his work. I like a face to look like a face. Like in a photo. And I'm thinking there was one missing today."

Caroline spoke over her, "Splendid. Why don't we all go back to Chiltern Hall, and I'll make us afternoon tea? Hayley, you go to fetch Terry and Betty. And would Abigail, Suzie, and Lillian like to come back in the Jag with me?"

So it was that the chauffeur looked in his mirror and saw her ladyship deep in conversation, but not with him. But he had worked for the aristocracy for forty years now, and nothing surprised him anymore.

Mrs Bittens, the old housekeeper, met Lady Caroline as she entered the Hall to see her talking to herself and gesturing to come to the drawing room. She figured either she was going doolally or her ladyship was. But she didn't say a word and agreed to serve afternoon tea for two in an hour. Cucumber sandwiches and her excellent Victorian sponge would be perfect. The rich were affectionately called eccentric, whereas the likes of her would be called bonkers. Oh well, it wasn't her place to ask questions.

But Mrs Bittens felt better when she let her ladyship's friend, Hayley, in. Although she had seen her talking to herself on the odd occasion. She shook her head as she went back to the kitchen, thinking how unfair life was that the ones she worked for were all a bit weird, but they were the ones with the money and lands.

"Hayley," said Caroline, "come and sit down next to me. Are the others all here? If not, I've been talking to myself for the last hour."

"Yes, you have the whole Deadly Detective Agency here. Terry and Betty couldn't see Fiona anywhere, so hopefully, she's moved on. They're saying they would love to have some of the lovely cake. But I suppose I'll have to eat their share."

"I think you're allowed to. I heard you can eat for two when you're pregnant."

"Trouble is, sometimes I'm eating for four."

"How much longer have you got?"

"About six weeks. I can't wait and don't think this little one can either. He's very active. I have a feeling he'll be quite a handful once he's born. Mum said I was a dreadful sleeper when I was young. Not just as a baby, but until I was about seven. I was forever getting in bed with them. As I got bigger, she always sent me out. They never believed me when I said there was someone in my room. Especially not after me saying I'd seen a big black shadow or the ghost of a lady. At least I'll be more understanding."

"They never believed you?"

"Never. It was only when I went to stay with my Nan, and she believed me and let me sleep in with her, that I understood. She had the gift too."

"Is that the one where you went to stay on the farm?"

"No, that was my dad's parents. This was Mum's mum."

"And you think your son will inherit the gift too?"

"Yes. I'm not sure if it's a gift, though. If it is, I'd have liked to give it back most of the time. But you can't, can you? I think Mum is psychic too, but she chose to try and ignore it."

"When do you think Benjie will show the first signs?"

"Nan said as soon as I could sit up, I'd be looking over to where she could see a shadow, and I'd be jabbering away. She was convinced it was her dad, who had passed away a few years before. Then I was about one when I'd wake up screaming. Mum said they were just night terrors."

"She wasn't wrong," said Suzie. "Sounds awful."

Caroline said, "Tom's got a lot to get used to, hasn't he?"

"He has, hun. I'll try and keep as much from him as I can. And half the stuff he won't want to know anyway. But Benjie will never be made to feel like a freak like I was at times. I'll always protect him in this life and after. I'll always be there, watching on both sides."

Abigail, in her blunt way, told them to stop nattering and get back to the subject of the murders. Or, as she called it—The Case of the Deadly Wedding.

"Sorry, Caroline, bossy boots here is telling us to get back to the murders."

"Abigail?"

"How does she know it's me? It could have been anyone. But fair point, I suppose."

Lillian said, "What gets my goat is that if it's Darren Kaye, that means Johnson is right. He always says it's the husband. All we've done is prove him right. Dave did tell Tom that he had a very attractive receptionist."

"But I'm not sure I was right when I said it was Saloni's husband now. I know, Terry, it's very unusual that I'm wrong. Let me go through it again to make sure."

Abigail leaned back once more, closed her eyes, and moved her hands as if she were moving chess pieces. This time, new pieces were forming in her mind.

"That might be it, maybe," she said to herself.

"Abigail said she might have got it, Caroline. I'll pass it on to you as quietly as I can. She's gone to stand in front of the fireplace. She likes to do that. It's her inner Poirot."

"Don't worry, Hayley, I'll go and get us some more tea, and you can tell me in one go afterwards. It will be much easier all round," and Caroline went to find Mrs Bittens.

"Right, Abi, is it Darren Kaye?" asked Terry.

"I know it is," said Lillian. "He altered the time of death, didn't he? And then his girlfriend covered for him."

"I think it's Daniel," said Betty. "I knew he was a cheating ba—"

"No. Ladies and gentlemen, I now know it wasn't Darren Kaye," Abigail pronounced dramatically. None of them looked convinced.

"Come on, dear, don't keep us in suspenders."

"I can't quite believe it myself. I'm just going on instinct, really. But there were three things that I heard and saw yesterday and again today that pointed me in the right direction. Someone lied about where they went after the meal, and I know why. I saw the truth of that in the photographs. After you had spoken to Tom yesterday, you said something that I took no notice of until now—the fact that people were standing outside the Great Hall smoking. And when you were talking about Benjie just now, you gave me the biggest clue of all."

"Did I? I can't think what."

"Isn't she marvellous," said Suzie. "I could listen to her all day."

"The way she's going on, we probably will be," said Terry.

"I'm getting there. Don't be so impatient. First, I just need you to check something, Hayley. Could you ring Amelia's number and see if Daniel is there?"

"Told you," said Betty.

"I want you to ask him one question." Abigail whispered something to Hayley.

Hayley called and spoke to Amelia. "How are you doing, hun? I'm so sorry. I won't keep you. Have you got company? Good. I just need to ask Daniel one quick question. Hello, Daniel. Sorry to disturb you, but I need to know one thing. Yes, it is very important. What was the name of Ava and Eve's mother?"

"Pippa? Thank you very much."

Chapter 22

"Oh my God, I can't believe you're right, hun. Pippa was the mother of Ava and Eve," said Hayley. "So you're saying—actually, what are you saying?"

"Pippa was killed by her husband, Ava and Eve's father—George. I should have noticed yesterday when you said you couldn't wait to help Pippa. In her letter, she had written that she wanted someone to take care of her baby girls."

"But George told Johnson that his wife had died three years ago," said Terry.

"We don't know how many wives he's got through, do we? Then when Hayley said she would help Benjie in life and death, that really got me thinking. And of course, the timing of her noticing the painting must have meant something.

Now, on Saturday, we were there when George told Johnson that he had given up smoking and was now addicted to e-cigarettes. Three things came from that: the painting had a brown layer of nicotine on it, he wasn't in that photo that Philip had taken of the smokers outside after the meal, and what better way to store a liquid poison than in the nicotine part of one of those cigarettes? He just told the police he went for one if they saw it in his pocket if they searched everyone. Of course, he couldn't risk taking a puff of it. They might have checked if he had it in a bottle of nicotine, so he had to put it in the actual e-cigarette itself.

But what was the reason, you're asking? If we assume he killed Pippa, there could be a pattern to it. What if he killed Pippa for her life insurance?

Darren Kaye said Saloni had recognised someone. Philip said he went to Amelia's for his appointment as it was easier, so Saloni could have seen George there, and he recognised her."

"Ah, so he was a bigamist?" said Terry.

"No, worse than that. I think he was a widower again. Tom can probably find out if he got married after Pippa died and before he met Fiona. Must have been quite a while ago when she was at the baker's in Gorebridge. I think George was already planning Fiona's murder, so another death would have been hard for him to explain. It'll be interesting to find out if the house and the money are in Fiona's name. Might even be another life insurance payout. So when he realised that he needed to shut Saloni up in case she remembered him, he had the brilliant idea of incorporating a serial killer. I think it's ingenious—if it wasn't so brutal, of course. Killing two birds with four bushes, as Betty says."

"So if you're right, you're saying George killed five people, hun? That nice-looking man?"

"It does seem a bit unbelievable now I've said it out loud."

"Have we got any proof? Sorry, a painting with a letter from goodness knows who is hardly a smoking gun," said Hayley. "Oh no, hun, I've just remembered something. It can't be George. Remember, when we were leaving Amelia's, the parents were coming in the door. He was with them, so he couldn't have been in Becklesfield attacking Mrs Merry. We went straight there, and it had just happened."

"Um, let me think." Abigail closed her eyes again for a few

seconds. "But if you remember, he came in last and said hello, but what if he was talking to the others as well and was just meeting up with his wife? He said he'd grabbed the red wine for the meal, so he might have said he was going to the shop to get some. When we got back, the police weren't there yet, so he'd have had ample time to get back."

"There might just have been time. So what do we need Tom to find out?"

"He needs to check if George got married after Pippa. I think it will not be long after she died. The daughters will probably have been young enough that they don't remember. But not longer than ten years ago before Saloni worked in Gorebridge. Then he needs to find out if he had life insurance on her."

"I'll go and find Caroline and then ring Tom."

"Oh, and ask Caroline if she fancies another visit. I think she should go with you and pay her condolences to George. Being a close friend of Fiona, of course. He'll never know."

"Are you sure that's wise, Abigail?" said Lillian after Hayley had left the room.

"He's hardly likely to do anything. And Suzie will be there. Besides, he thinks he's got away with it. He'd never think two women could be as clever as him."

Betty said, "He's what they call a missausages."

"What's that?" asked Suzie.

"It means he doesn't like women, dear."

"I'll be there anyway. I'll pick up something and hit him on the head if he tries to hurt either of them," added Suzie, while lifting her hand and bringing it down with force.

"And I'll be there. There are some questions I need to ask him. Imagine if I'm wrong—how stupid Hayley will look in front of Johnson. We owe it to her."

So an hour later, after getting the address from a surprised Amelia, they knocked at the door of a beautiful thatched cottage on the edge of Featheridge.

Hayley wasn't sure if it was Ava or Eve who had answered the door.

"Do you remember me from the wedding? I was wondering if your father was in. Tell him it's Hayley Bennett and Lady Caroline Hatton. We want to say how sorry we are for your loss."

George walked out of the living room. "Come in, please. Did you know my wife, Lady Hatton, did you say?" Hayley felt his eyes light up as he thought he might have met wife number four.

"Yes, I had met your wife at a few charity events."

"Really? I wasn't aware she did much for charities."

"Oh, off and on, you know."

"These are my daughters, Ava and Eve." The two young girls were sitting watching television and looked even more miserable when their father turned it off with the control.

"Sit down. I'm not quite sure why you've come. Not that I'm not honoured."

"When my friend, Hayley, told me what had happened, I just had to say how sorry I was and give my condolences from everyone at the Women's Institute."

"I hope you're not thinking of the wrong Fiona." George knew that he would never let Fiona join anything like that. He never let her go anywhere without him. He'd made sure she never saw her brother even. If he could have, he would have stopped her seeing that useless son, Daniel. But whatever he told her about him—his infidelities or laziness—she would never think badly of him. But he made sure she didn't have any friends since they'd been married. And she wouldn't have dared to go behind his back. Even going to the supermarket, he timed her. And God help her if she was too long or got anything that wasn't on the list he'd written.

"I'm sure she used to help with the cake sales," said Caroline.

"Perhaps she did then."

"The girls must be devastated to lose their mother in such a sudden way."

"They are, Lady Hatton. It was a terrible thing for anyone to see."

"She wasn't our mother," said Eve, the older of the two.

George looked angrily at her. "But she was like a mother to them."

"I'm sorry you've been through this twice. When did she pass, George?"

"When they were little. Fortunately, they don't remember her death."

"And then you met Fiona. When was that?"

"I'm sorry, is there a reason to bring back all those memories? I have just lost my wife."

Caroline said, "I was just wondering if we could help with the funeral arrangements. I have a friend who could do the catering—on me, of course. Or anything else you can think of."

"Excuse me for just a moment, George. I'd better take this, it's my husband calling," said Hayley as she went out into the entrance hall. "Go on, hun, what did you find out?" she whispered.

"I don't know how you did it, but you were right. George Arnold married Grace Ford seven years ago at Gorebridge Registry Office. She's got a sister, Clara, who hasn't seen her for years and had her named as a missing person. Apparently, Grace stopped all contact after the wedding. Said she wanted to get on with her life. Her sister thought it had something to do with him. She said he was awful. Nice to start with, but then got jealous, even if she rang her up. Clara stopped bothering, and when she tried to get in touch one birthday, he told her that Grace couldn't cope with the children and had left him. Clara has no idea where her sister is."

"I think I do," said Hayley. "She can't be alive."

"And if she did have life insurance, he didn't claim it. I'll tell you why—he didn't need to. She had a lot of money of her own. Both she and Clara had inherited half a million each from an uncle. Sounds like you're right. So be careful. Leave it to the police. I've already talked to Dave, and he's sorting out a warrant. Where are you now?"

"Ah, now don't be angry…"

"Oh, Hayley, you'd better not be. You're there at his house? Oh my God. Make an excuse and get out of there fast. I'm on my way."

Hayley turned to see George behind her.

Chapter 23

"Girls, go to your room. UPSTAIRS, NOW!" George shouted.

Caroline, looking confused, said, "What's happened? Hayley?" while Abigail was screaming at them to run.

"I've just found your friend getting a report from her policeman husband. Sit down, please. I'm not going to hurt you. Not yet, anyway. Hayley has just found out that I was married before I met Fiona. So what? I may or may not be a bigamist. It's hardly the crime of the century. I loved Fiona so much that I couldn't wait to find out where Grace was, so we married. Grace left me when the kids were small. She couldn't cope with suddenly having such young girls to look after, so she walked out one day. I was too ashamed to tell anyone."

"We all know she didn't leave you."

"Do we? Do we really?"

Abigail said, "Don't goad him, Hayley. Suzie, get ready to pick up that candlestick."

"It was her money, wasn't it? We can soon check if she took her money with her. And if she's been spending it," said Hayley shakily.

"You won't find it in my account. She was very depressed, so I wouldn't be surprised if she took her own life."

Abigail said to ask her about Pippa while he was so talkative.

"Tell me about Pippa. How did she die?"

"How the hell do you know about Pippa? I don't suppose it will hurt to tell you. We got married and had the two girls. And when they were still very young, Pippa, unfortunately, was carrying the washing down the stairs when she fell. She'd trod on the duvet cover and lost her footing. Went headfirst down the stairs and died instantly." George put his hand on his heart. "I was devastated."

"So devastated that you married a rich, older lady."

"Love has no time schedule and isn't governed by age, Hayley. Besides, the girls needed a mother, so we had a quick ceremony."

"But you didn't reckon on seeing Saloni again at Danny's when she came about the cake, did you?"

"Grace and I had a small wedding at a registry office. Just Clara, her sister, and a few friends. We had the reception at the local, and she wanted a nice wedding cake. It was very tasty, if I remember correctly. Whether she recognised me, I don't know. But if she did, that would be very annoying. Especially if, as you're insinuating—quite wrongly, of course—that I killed my first wife as well as planning on doing away with Fiona. I might be guilty of bigamy, but even that—you'd need to find Grace alive to be sure. I'll take my chances."

"Perhaps they'll find the poison in the e-cigarette."

"My, you and your imagination have been busy. So I am responsible for Fiona's death as well, am I? And the others? Surely you know, if what you say is true, that I'd be clever enough to get rid of any evidence."

"There's always something. You've tripped yourself up somewhere."

"There's no proof of anything. And I hate to tell you, but I have alibis for everything. For the attack on that poor florist in Becklesfield, I was with you at Daniel's. Becklesfield—that's where you live, isn't it?" he said with a threatening smirk.

"You could have done it before you got there. When you were getting the wine."

"Is that right? When is the baby due? I hope you get to nine months. It would be awful if anything happened."

Suzie shouted, "Let me whack him, Abigail." But luckily for him, they all heard the sound of sirens getting closer.

"Lady Hatton, thank you for your kind offer, but I'm afraid I will have to pass. It seems I will be a bit tied up for the next few days. A shame all your ideas are just fantasy. There's not one bit of proof—maybe for the bigamy, but I'll take my chances. But I'll be in touch as soon as I can, Hayley. Now, please excuse me, I'd better open the front door before they break it down."

Chapter 24

"Sorry, Hayl, we had to let him go. We couldn't keep him in custody longer than twenty-four hours," Tom told Hayley when he got home the next night.

"I can't believe he's going to get away with all those deaths. Can't we get him for one of them?"

"His first wife's death, Pippa, was ruled an accidental death, and she was cremated. There's no body or proof that Grace is dead, although she hasn't used her credit card or bank account since she left. We'll be looking into that, though. If you're right about Pippa being scared of him, Grace might have run away somewhere he couldn't find her."

"I know, hun, but I have a dreadful feeling about Grace. What about the other deaths?"

"For Saloni's, he was with a female customer. He's some sort of accountant. We can't get her to change her statement. Mind you, she could be lying from fear or a bribe. When Miriam was stabbed with those scissors, he was at home with Fiona and the girls. He says he was doing the gardening. Ava and Eve swear they heard the mower going when he wasn't inside."

"He could have kept the motor running. Put it on bricks or something."

"Maybe. Going to be hard to prove, though. We showed his picture to the lady who sold the scissors in that haberdashery, but she couldn't say if it was him. And you saw him the day of Mrs Merry's attack. He could have done it, but it would have been tight for time, and no one saw him in Becklesfield. But if he went in the back way, they wouldn't have. There's no physical evidence at his house, like blood on his clothes or shoes. He's good, I'll give him that. No one saw him put poison in Fiona's glass. It's up to the CPS to say if they are going to charge him with bigamy. His lawyer is convinced they haven't got a case. He's saying he had given her divorce papers and she was going to sign them. Chances are it will be a hefty fine and no jail time. He's got an answer for everything. The only consolation is that if he wasn't really married to Fiona, he won't be entitled to her money. But it could be that the house is in both their names by now."

"So when Pippa died and he met Grace, did they live in his house?" asked Hayley.

"Yes, Grace moved into his house with the two young girls. He sold it when he met Fiona, and they all moved into her beautiful cottage. Daniel had already moved in with Amelia. It's got to be worth a few million in that area. Good motive, isn't it? And Fiona was insured for another million. And when we asked Daniel if his mother had ever suffered from seizures or was ill, he said she hadn't been to the doctors for years. That would have made it hard to make it look like a heart attack or a stroke. And another fall would have been suspicious. No wonder he came up with the crazed killer idea."

"It's not right. I worry for his daughters. I promised Pippa I would look after them."

"We'll keep an eye on them. They didn't seem to be frightened of him. But they probably wouldn't dare say if he's as bad as we think. They couldn't tell us much. Eve, the older one—she's thirteen, I think—said she can remember a lady living with them for a while, but then one day she'd gone."

"That's one way of putting it. That has to be Grace. Did Eve remember the wedding?"

"No. He must have kept it from them. Let's face it, if he knew he was going to kill her from the start, he wouldn't have wanted them asking questions. It's not easy to explain away a wife. They're fine at the moment. They're staying with Amelia and Daniel. Don't worry about them."

"I feel sorry for him as well. We thought it might have been him for a while. Hopefully, this will make Daniel grow up and he'll realise how lucky he is."

"I just hope he doesn't take matters into his own hands. He really believes his stepdad is capable of killing his mum. Apparently, she made a few comments, and once he saw bruises on her wrists. It's easy to spot the signs with hindsight."

"It sure is, hun. I'm really exhausted, Tom. I think I'll go up and have a read. I got a new book from the library the other day."

"Yeah, go on. I'll empty the dishwasher and join you."

Hayley was asleep within ten minutes of getting in bed, with Luna stretched out next to her. That only left a quarter of the bed for Tom, but he got in carefully and fell asleep too. That was until he heard a scream from the other side of the bed.

"What's up? Is the baby coming? I'll get the case. Where is it? I can't find it. Or should I time the contractions? Where's my watch? We really need to get rid of all this junk. Where are the car keys?"

"Tom. Tom. Come back. It's not the baby. I promise. Relax. I had a nightmare, that's all."

"Why didn't you say that?"

"You didn't give me a chance. You were too busy panicking."

"Sorry, love. Sorry, Luna," he said, getting back in bed.

"And it's not junk, it's the baby stuff. We really need to do the nursery. Trouble is, that is still full of junk. I'll try and sort it out tomorrow. And I think we ought to have a trial run if I go into labour at night after what I just saw. Sorry, Tom, you were pretty useless."

"Well, it was my first attempt," he laughed. "Thank God it wasn't for real. Do you want to tell me about the dream? It might help."

"You usually fall asleep before I've finished."

"I promise to listen this time. Well, I'll try."

"I was looking at myself and my whole face changed into someone else. Then I suddenly turned into a skull. That's when I woke up. It was horrible. Even for me."

"It was just a dream. Wasn't it?"

"I hope so, hun."

"Where were you?"

"I'm not sure. Nowhere I know. I was looking at myself, so I didn't notice anything else."

"Were you having an out-of-body thing?"

"I have no idea. It's got to mean something, though."

"Not necessarily. It could be your brain reacting to Fiona's death. You feel guilty for that, even though you shouldn't. Maybe it's her one minute, and then she's turned into a skeleton."

"I don't think it was Fiona, but you're right, I've got to let it go. I'm sure the police will get him in the end. Let's face it, we've got enough to do. We need to clear the spare room and then paint it. What colour do you think?"

But Tom was already sleeping, or he was pretending to. He did seem to drift off when Hayley suggested painting the nursery. Luna, however, was meowing and looking expectantly at his mother for a snack. It was the least she could do after waking him up in the middle of the night.

"Sorry, Luna. You've got as much chance of getting an invitation from the dog next door to go for afternoon tea. But I promise I'll give you extra treats, and maybe we'll have cuddles in bed after I've bagged up some of the junk to go to the charity shop. Settle down, Daddy has got work in the morning. Poor Daddy."

Luna had just drifted off and was dreaming of chasing a huge ball of wool when she woke him up again. This time she was muttering that she knew what it was. Humans were very strange.

Chapter 25

AS SOON AS THE LIBRARIAN UNLOCKED THE DOOR, Hayley swept past her as she said good morning. Thirty seconds later, she flew past her again, saying she had to go. Even for her, the librarian thought it was strange behaviour, and she had seen her laugh and talk to herself on many occasions.

Lillian, Suzie, and Terry had left early, so it was just Abigail and Betty who followed the animated Hayley out the door. She didn't care who thought she looked crazy as she walked briskly down the high street.

"Hold up, Hayley. Is it the baby? Is our Benjie coming?" shouted Abigail.

"Why do people always think that? No, come over here. I've got something to tell you that will blow your hats off. Where can we talk without me getting carted off? The swings—come on."

"If it's not the baby, what is it, dear? We know that man has been released. We heard it from the late Archie Crosswell that they can't charge him. We're so sorry. But we'll be watching him like a horse," said Betty gently.

"I know, but it's not that," Hayley said excitedly. "Abigail, do you remember when we went to the charity shop to get my outfit for the wedding, and that was the first time I'd noticed the painting of the windmill?"

"Of course I do."

"And I saw that mirror that I said I was too scared to look in, as my reflection wasn't there?"

"Yes. It was a room you didn't recognise. What about it?"

"It came to me last night after a dream of looking at myself. Tom and I were talking about clearing the junk out of the nursery, and I suddenly thought that maybe the painting and the mirror had both come from the same place. Tom told me that George had lived in Pippa's house after he married Grace, but when he married Fiona, he sold it a few years ago. Now, he would have had to clear the house, and Mr Harding said it had come as part of a house clearance. What if they were both from George's house?"

"Nothing would surprise me. But you said the mirror was evil, and you wouldn't have it in the house with the baby."

"I still think it holds something evil, but I'm going to buy it. I have to see what it's trying to show me. That could be what's malevolent, not the actual mirror. Oh, I hope Mr Harding hasn't sold it. Come on."

"Morning, Hayley. How was the wedding? Oh, sorry, I forgot. But at least the dress looked nice, I hope."

"It did. I saw some photos yesterday, and I looked rather nice. But ... oh no, where's the mirror that I saw when I was in here? It was there."

"It's still here somewhere. After we looked at it, I noticed it had come from a smoker's house, so I gave it a wipe. The brass came up like new. There it is."

Hayley kept her eyes on the frame, not daring to see its secrets yet. "How much is it?"

"It's got that crack on the corner, so would ten pounds be alright?"

The Deadly Wedding

"Brilliant. Will it go in a carrier bag, do you think?"

"Er, just. There you are. It could be an antique, you know. Mrs Myrtle was going to buy it, but she got a funny feeling about it—like someone had walked over her grave."

"How strange. But if I do, I'll donate it back to you. I've got some stuff of my own to bring over tomorrow."

"The animals and the birds thank you very much. Enjoy your mirror."

Hayley didn't think that was the right word for what she had to do. She told the two ghosts that she would definitely not be taking it back home, so they decided to go and sit in the churchyard on the old wooden bench.

"Right, here goes nothing," said Hayley, crossing herself. "At least we get a bit of protection on consecrated ground."

She slid it out of the plastic bag and closed her eyes. She steadied it on her lap and took a deep breath. She took a chance and stared deep into the centre of the glass.

The ever-impatient Abigail said, "So what can you see?"

"Hang on, it's got mist over it. It's clearing now. Well, I can't see me. Can you see me?"

"Yes, it's just a normal mirror to us."

"The mist is going now. I see a room. It's a bedroom. Flowery wallpaper on the walls. A bed that hasn't been slept in. A dressing table. It's like looking in a window. There's someone sitting at the dressing table, brushing their light brown hair. I hear a door opening. She doesn't turn round. There's a man in a blue jumper. Oh my God, I think it's George. He's saying, 'Grace, I've got a surprise for you.' She's turned around now. 'For me?' 'Yes. To say sorry for yesterday. I'm going to put in a pond at the bottom of the garden.' Grace says, 'What a lovely idea. What are you going to put in it?' 'You'. Oh my God, I can't look. He's got his hands around her throat, and he's squeezing. He's choking her to death. He's smiling. Please stop it, I can't stand it."

Abigail and Betty both put their arms around her. "You must see it to the end, Hayley," said Abigail. "For Grace and all the others."

"I know, I know. He's taking a bedspread off the bed and laying it on the floor. I can't believe it—he's wrapping her in it and dragging her towards the door. It's gone. All I can see is me."

Hayley dropped it on the grass and burst into tears. She had dealt with murder before, but this was the cruellest thing she had ever witnessed. There was nothing Betty or Abigail could do to console her.

Reverend Pete Stevens was making his way from the vicarage to the church when he came across his friend and parishioner sitting on her own in floods of tears.

"Hayley, what's happened? It's not the baby, is it?"

"No, the baby is fine. I've just got a lot on my mind at the moment."

"It's a worrying time with your first, but you and Tom will be great parents."

"I know, Pete. It's not that. Although, when I see all the evil in the world, I wonder if we're even doing the right thing in having one."

"People have been thinking that for hundreds of years, and we're still going. I like to think that there are far more people who do kindness than evil. And if anyone can protect your baby, it's you and Tom. I'll remind you of this in five years' time when your little one is running around and bringing you all sorts of joy like you've never imagined. And the Church will always be here for you. Is that your mirror?"

"Yes, I just bought it from the charity shop. It's what's depressed me."

"You just look tired, that's all."

Hayley had to laugh. "Oh, now I look old and haggard as well."

"I didn't mean that, silly. Why don't you come back to the vicarage, and we'll have a cup of tea with Mary?"

"There's something I need to do first. Maybe tomorrow if I can. Although, goodness knows, I haven't got the time. We haven't even finished decorating the nursery yet. And Tom never has the time to build all the baby stuff. I do have a favour, though—could you take this mirror and look after it in the church? I'll collect it when I know what to do with it. I'll put it in the bag."

"Of course. I'll put it safely in the vestry. Do you want me to walk home with you?"

"No, thank you. You've actually made me feel a lot better."

Hayley walked slowly home, accompanied by Abigail and Betty. None of them talked like they usually did. And when Hayley got back, she did something that she had never done before.

Instead of ringing Tom, she rang Sergeant Mills. She told him that she had information from an anonymous source who said that Grace Arnold was buried under a pond in George's old house, where his wife, Pippa had fallen to her death. Grace had been strangled and wrapped in a purple bedspread. May she now rest in peace.

Two weeks later, Hayley went into the library waving the Chiltern Weekly. It was the article they had been waiting for. There were enough people in there to not take any notice of a heavily pregnant woman reading out loud from a newspaper at the back of the library.

Grim find in Upper Danford

The body of a woman was found under the concrete of a pond following a tip-off.

It is thought to be the body of fifty-four-year-old Grace Arnold. Her sister, Clara Lane, told the Chiltern Weekly that she had been missing for seven years. "I'm just so relieved to know what happened to her at last. I knew she wouldn't have gone without keeping in touch with me."

A man has been arrested who is thought to be her husband, George Arnold, aged forty-seven. His current wife, Fiona, died at Micklebrook Priory under suspicious circumstances on March 10th. It is not known if the two deaths are connected. Fiona's son, Daniel, said, "I hope my mother gets the justice she deserves. We are all brokenhearted, and our lives will never be the same again."

At a news conference, Detective Chief Inspector Johnson of Gorebridge CID told us,

"It is by good police work that we have given closure to the family of Grace. Enquiries are ongoing into several other cases connected to the so-called 'Something Borrowed Murders'."

We'll keep you updated as soon as we have more information.

"That's marvellous, Hayley. I bet you feel a lot better today."

"Oh, Terry, I really do. As soon as Tom said they'd found Grace, I felt a huge weight lifted off my shoulders."

"I love how they are calling it the Something Borrowed Murders. That was my idea. Actually, they might never have known if I hadn't thought of it."

"You're right, Abigail. Wouldn't it be great if they could have put that in the paper?"

"We know how brilliant you are," said Suzie. "You're as good as the ones in these books. And they aren't even dead. Imagine how good you'd be if you were alive."

"I know, what a waste. But if I was, I'd be turning up trousers and putting zips in probably. If I had my life again, I don't think I'd join the police. I've seen how many hours Tom has to work. I'd start a detective agency."

Suzie said, "What's that thing when you're born again? You could do that."

"Reincarnation. Mind you, I don't think I'd want to go through childhood again. I'd like to go straight to being eighteen. It's when you look your best and every bit of your body is where it should be. And you can go to the pub and drink. It is what it is, though. I'm dead, and you just have to make the best of things."

Betty said, "Always look on the bright side of death."

"Today is a good day anyway," said Hayley. "But now this is over, I need to go and sort the nursery out. If I went into labour now, I'd have to put poor Benjie in the laundry basket."

"I'll come and help," said Suzie.

"I'll come too and tell you what to do," said Abigail.

"Sounds about right. Come on then."

As the three of them turned into Church Lane, Hayley was shocked to see a group of people outside her house. Had something happened? She recognised Reverend Pete and Mary, and as she got closer, she saw Bill Bates, Joyce Blair, and two villagers she didn't know well.

"Is everything okay? I haven't forgotten something, have I?"

Mary came towards her and held both of her hands. "No, but we've got a surprise for you. You and Tom have always done so much for the village, and so we want to pay you back for all your kindness."

"Really?"

"We know Tom has been busy with work and you haven't felt your best, so when Pete asked on Sunday if anyone wanted to help you do the nursery, he was overwhelmed with offers. We had to turn a lot of people down. So Bill is going to lay new carpet, Joyce and her daughter are going to paint, and we've got more than enough volunteers to build the cot and baby's furniture. We thought cream carpet and pale yellow walls, if that's okay? Janette at the library has a day off and has offered to babysit Luna at her house, so everything is arranged. You just say what needs to be taken out, and we'll do the rest."

"I could cry, that's amazing. Thank you. I was just saying the baby will have to sleep in the laundry basket. I've sorted all the rubbish out in there. I've got bags for the dump, a couple for recycling, and a couple of boxes for the charity shop. I can't thank you enough."

"You don't have to. It's us that are thanking you," said Pete. "Is there anywhere you could go while we're doing it? I don't want the paint fumes to get on your chest."

"I have got a chore that I need to do. I've been putting it off for days, if you don't mind. And as soon as I get back, I'll pick up some buns from the shop and make you all a cup of tea. But first, Pete, I have another favour."

"Anything for you, Hayley."

Hayley pulled up outside and wondered if she was doing the right thing. It was too late now—she'd already phoned ahead and said she was coming. She didn't want any of the agency with her when she did this. She wanted it to be a calm, precious moment. She picked up her bag and walked up the drive.

"Hi, Hayley, come in. Did you see the news conference on the television last night?" asked Amelia.

"I did. I read about it in the paper today as well. How is Daniel?"

"Hovering between being in pieces and at boiling point. If he could get near George, he'd kill him. He can't believe his mum was with a monster for all those years. And when I think of the times George came around here, honestly, I feel ill. Anyway, enough about us—how are you and the baby doing?"

"I think I'm getting really close. And I'm so blessed that some of the neighbours are painting the nursery for us and building the baby furniture. It's put my faith back in humanity. I think that's why the vicar has arranged it. When I saw him last, I told him I wasn't sure if I wanted to bring up a baby in this world."

"What's happened lately isn't going to put me off starting a family. In fact, it's made me more determined to enjoy life while I can."

"You've got a family now, I hear. Tom said Ava and Eve are going to live with you."

"They've been so good. I think they're quite pleased they don't have to live with him anymore. They won't say what they saw over the years, but one day they might."

"They will when they learn to trust again. They're lucky to have you."

"You said you have something for the girls. You needn't worry. I know they had to leave a lot of their stuff there, but the police say we can get it. And we've bought them a whole new wardrobe. Luckily, the only thing they seem to need is a TV and their computer games. And a few teddies."

"It's nothing like that. I can't explain it all, but you know what I do?"

"Of course."

"Well, I found these in a charity shop, and Pete just gave me one of them back that he had been looking after. Now, I can't say exactly how I know, but they both belonged to the girls' mother, Pippa. It's how I worked out that it was George in the end. And where to find the body of Grace. One day, I might be able to tell you the whole truth."

"That was you? Oh my God, wait till I tell everyone."

"That's just it—you can't. I don't need people laughing or, worse still, a load of journalists asking me awkward questions. You've got to promise this stays between us."

"If I must." She had already decided she would tell Danny. And make him swear to keep it secret, of course. And Mum for sure. "So what have you got for them?"

Hayley pulled out the painting and then the mirror. "The mirror hung in Pippa's bedroom. I'm not sure about the painting."

"Let me see. Oh my God, that's a Rowena Raven."

"I know. Have you heard of her? I hadn't."

"You do remember I studied Art at uni and own a gallery. A Raven is worth a lot of money these days."

"No. How much? No, don't tell me. Okay, how much?"

"We sold one for two thousand pounds. Still want to give it to the girls? How much did you pay for it?"

"Twenty-five pounds. Blimey. But no, I think Pippa would have wanted it to go to her girls. I hope the oldest one, Eve I think, remembers it."

"Let's find out. Girls, could you come here for a minute?"

The two fair-haired girls walked shyly into the room. They recognised the lady from the night that Daddy was arrested for the first time. That was the night they came to live with Amelia and Daniel. It was so nice not to be scared for the first time.

"I'm Hayley, we met once before. I've got something for you. I sort of knew your mother, and when I came across these two things, I knew she would want you to have them. You might not remember them, but you should still have them."

Amelia handed over the painting to Eve. She stared at it and then looked like she was about to cry as she rubbed a finger over it.

"Mummy loved this. She had it in the kitchen. She used to tell us how she went to the windmill with her nanny and grandad. She said it wasn't there anymore."

The Deadly Wedding

"That's right. I went with some friends to see where it was."

"Perhaps Danny and I could take you on Sunday. We could take a picnic if it's warm enough. Do you remember it, Ava?"

"No. I wish I did. I don't remember Mummy at all."

"I know she loved you very much and will always think of you. And I found this mirror. I think it used to hang in her bedroom."

Eve said, "It was on her chest of drawers. It used to have a stand on the back. I could lift it off and hold it while Mummy brushed my hair. And yours, Ava. She said we should brush our hair a hundred times every night. But we never got that far. I can almost feel her doing it. Then she'd carry you, and I'd walk to our room. She'd tickle my neck until I fell asleep. I'd forgotten that. Can we keep them in our room, please?"

"Of course, they're yours now. Off you go," said Amelia.

"Bless them. That went well. I don't know why I was worrying so much."

"Do you think I should tell them how much the painting is worth?" said Amelia.

"To be honest, I think it's worth far more than money to them. They seem quite happy, considering."

"We don't know what their dad was really like behind closed doors. I bet they had to walk on eggshells. We'll make sure they have therapy if they need it. I think Daniel might need to see someone in the future."

"And you. Don't forget yourself."

"What about you? How are you feeling, Hayley?"

"I'm getting there. I have no idea why the neighbours would offer to help."

"I know the reason; you're a good person, Hayley. Look at that painting. Most people would have thought better of that. And I'm sure you didn't want to come to my wedding with a load of people you didn't know, but you did."

"Not at all," lied Hayley. "And the meal was nice."

"Yes, at least we had that before, you know."

"Well, if you need any help with anything, let me know. If it helps, I see no more bad prophecies in your future, hun."

"Thank goodness for that. And next time, if you do, don't tell me!" said Amelia.

That evening, Hayley sat on the white nursing chair and felt a huge relief. They had done a wonderful job. Benjie's nursery looked like it could be in a baby magazine. Tom was even more pleased than her when he got home from work and said he didn't know how he could make it up to the neighbours.

"They don't want you to make it up to them. You have to accept it gracefully, with thanks and love."

"Well, I want to make sure they know how grateful we are."

"They do, and one day we'll show them, hun."

"They've done a much better job than we would have done."

"I know, right? You'd still be building the cot and changing table. And you'd be turning the air blue, but not with paint."

"It's perfect and looks so clean. Look at all the little clothes in the wardrobe. Surely he's not going to be that tiny, is he?"

"I'm new to this too, hun. It's going to be scary holding a baby, let alone putting one of those all-in-one suits on him. How does he even get in it?"

"Have you ever changed a nappy?" asked Tom.

"I'd like to say yes, but I haven't. It can't be that hard, surely."

"I have no idea. It's a good job Mum lives in the next village. She might have to move in with us."

"I'll be fine," said Hayley quickly. She hoped Tom was joking.

"We'd better have an early night tonight while we can still get eight hours."

"Good idea. And I've sorted out another problem today. I gave that windmill painting to Ava and Eve. And the mirror. I'll tell you about that another time. So I think we'll both sleep well tonight."

But Benjie had other ideas, and much to Luna's annoyance, Hayley had a stabbing pain in her back when he was in his deepest sleep.

Benjamin Michael Bennett was born in Gorebridge General Hospital at 7.27 am. He weighed 7 pounds and 7 ounces. Mother and baby were both doing well. Father was exhausted.

Chapter 26

THAT NIGHT, AS ONE SOUL ENTERED THE WORLD, another one departed. The man was confused and beginning to think that he was dead. How had that happened? He was even more confused when a young man told him that if he went to the Becklesfield Public Library, there was a group of ghosts that could help him—adding that he should go at night because the librarian was threatening to call an exorcist. It was beginning to get light, so he made his way there quickly.

So, as Hayley was holding Benjamin for the first time, the newest Dead was warily approaching Abigail, Terry, and Betty. They knew immediately why he was there. He was dressed in a plaid shirt with jeans and had a beard and longish hair that was brushed back in a look that reminded Abigail of an old rock star.

"Can we help you?" asked Terry.

"You can, apparently. I just met a pilot, and he said to come here."

"That's Arthur. He used to fly Spitfires in the war. He usually sends the victims of violence here."

"Oh, I'm not sure I'm that."

"What else would you call that?" said Abigail bluntly. "They say the pen is mightier than the sword," she added, pointing to an old-fashioned fountain pen that was sticking out of his chest. "And it looks like you might have been punched on the chin. I'm sorry, but you had to know. Please, sit down."

"How did a pen get there? I have no idea. I can't think straight since I woke up. But then I haven't woken up."

"You have—you just woke up dead. I was the same. I'm Abigail, this is Betty, and this is Terry. You've come to the right place to find out. We're The Deadly Detective Agency. We're a bit down in numbers at the moment. We work with a medium, Hayley, and her policeman husband, but we've been told that she went to the hospital to have her baby in the night. So our nurse, Lillian, and little Suzie have gone to see what's happening. But don't worry about that. Start by telling us your name."

"Er, I think it's Carl Tonbridge."

"And who did this to you, dear?" asked Betty.

"If I knew, I'd tell you. I only know I was walking away from somewhere or something I didn't want to see."

"Do you think you could retrace your steps with us?"

"I could try. Can we go now?"

Betty said, "I'm going to stay here in case the others come back and tell us if Hayley has had the baby."

"So what are we looking for?" asked Carl.

"Your body, of course," said Abigail.

They turned left out of the village and headed past Ridgeway Wood, where they met Arthur, the pilot. He said he had seen Carl coming across the field from the west, but he couldn't say where from exactly. After the field, they went down a path lined on each side by a hedge.

"This leads to the canal," said Terry. "I used to cycle along it with my mates. Then we'd get on the bridge by the lock and go to Gorebridge. There's the bridge."

"It does look a bit familiar," said Carl.

"Well, you have definitely seen it today, I can tell you that," said Abigail.

"How do you know?"

"Because I don't think your name is Carl Tonbridge. Look—you saw that, and it got muddled in your mind."

"Carlton Bridge. Oh God, so who am I?"

Abigail walked down the towpath and stared into the murky water of the canal. "More to the point, where are you? You're not looking wet, so either you didn't go in the water, or you were dead before you did. See anything you recognise?"

"To be honest, no."

"What about those boats down there? We should check them out first." Terry had walked further round the bend and had seen two narrowboats tied up next to each other. They were both painted red with a green stripe at the top, and the hulls were black.

"If only Hayley was here. She could just knock and ask if you live on one of those," said Abigail.

"I'd like to think that I live in a big house, but you never know. I could have been walking or visiting. How do we find out if we can't ask them?"

"Being nosy has got us a long way in the past. Terry, go and have a look in that one."

Terry walked into the centre of the nearest barge, and they heard him shout, "Oh, I do apologise, miss. Oops," before stepping back out onto the path.

"What was she doing?"

"A gentleman never tells. The man was putting the kettle on, though. No body there, and they don't look the type to stab someone to death with a pen."

"Try that one, then. The curtains are pulled. That's never a good thing at this time of day."

The Deadly Wedding

Terry stepped down into the cockpit at the rear of the next boat and soon saw what they were looking for.

"He's in here! Sorry, mate, you might want to stay out there."

"No, I need to see it all. Perhaps I was here to see someone."

Carl, as they still called him, was lying on his back between the table and the sofa. He looked exactly the same, apart from not moving. His eyes and mouth were open in surprise.

Abigail pointed to a jacket that was on a chair. "I expect that's your coat. Looks like you came in and took it off. Everything else is put away. I suppose you have to be tidy in a small space like this. And your keys are on the table. I've just noticed that the main light isn't on in here, so you might not have had a good look at the person. Let's see if we can find anything with your name on it, if it is your boat. I wish Suzie was here to lift things. I'll just check your shoes. No, nothing to show where you've been—just grass and a bit of mud. Any luck, Terry?"

"There's this writing pad on the table, but nothing is written on the top page. Suzie could have looked at the others. But I'm betting it's been written on with a fountain pen. There's the ink."

"So it wasn't planned. Whoever it was punched you and then picked up whatever he could."

"What a horrible thought."

"I know, Carl. I was murdered as well. It does get better. Here's a waste bin full of paper, screwed up. Suzie could read that if we get her. Let's check the bedrooms first."

It was definitely Carl's boat. There was a photo of him with two small boys on either side of him in one of the berths.

"I don't even know them," he said sadly.

Abigail tapped his arm. "You will. They look like you, so you must be their dad."

"What do we do now? They've got to be told."

"It's a bit awkward. Usually, we'd tell Hayley. She's the only

Breather that can see us, and she'd tell her husband, who would think of a way of letting the other police know without involving her. I don't know what we should do."

"Nothing," said Terry. "We need to go to the library and get Suzie if she's back. She could do something to get attention. She was only nine when she died, Carl, and it only seems to be the young that can move things. Although, goodness knows how, because if she starts banging about, she could change the course of the investigation. Still, let's go back and see if there's any news of our gorgeous little godson yet."

Chapter 27

"IT'S A BOY," SHOUTED LILLIAN AS THE OTHERS GOT back from the canal. "He's perfect. He looks like Tom, but has Hayley's eyes and a big mop of black hair. We didn't let her see us. It should be their moment, but it's not like they can phone us, is it? And I'm sure she wouldn't mind. Sorry, who's this?"

"This is Carl, although we're not sure of his name yet. This is Lillian and Suzie. We found his body in a barge on the canal. But we've no way of letting anyone know."

"I could do that," said Suzie. "I'm so sorry you're dead. Have we met before? You look very familiar."

"I don't know. But I did see a lot of books on the boat, so maybe I came in here to get them. Or you might know my sons."

"I don't think it's that. I've definitely seen your face. Got it." Suzie ran off and disappeared from sight, like only a child can, and came running back holding a book.

"Look, this is you. You're not Carl, you're Trevor Grand. I've read all your books since I've been here. I'm the only one that can turn the pages."

"I'm an author?"

"Yes. You write murder mysteries about Detective Archer of Scotland Yard. Like The Perilous Picnic and The Dangerous Dalliance. Don't you remember?"

"No. I didn't even know my name was Trevor Grand. Doesn't sound like me. I don't feel like a Trevor."

"That might be a plom de nom or whatever it is," said Betty. "That's very good detective work, Suzie."

Abigail would have loved to have said how ironic it was to have a pen name, but thought it might be a bit soon.

"Thank you," said Suzie proudly. "There's usually an article about the author inside. Here it is. It says, Trevor Grand is an English author who lives in the Chiltern Hills. He is the author of the bestselling Inspector Archer series. He studied Literature at Bedford University and was in advertising until he signed with Wasp Sting Publishing and wrote the award-winning Inspector Archer Strikes. He is married with two children. When he is not writing, he loves to read and sail."

"I think that must have been written some time ago," said Trevor. "I don't think I'm married anymore. Or go sailing. Looks like she got the house and the yacht."

"We'll find all that out, don't worry," said Abigail. "Suzie, why don't you show Trevor what you can really do? Go with Terry and Lillian to the barge and do your stuff."

"Aren't you coming?" asked Terry.

"I never thought I'd say it, but there's more to death than murders; births in this case. Betty and I want to go and see our little Benjamin. I can't wait any longer."

Lillian pointed at her. "Don't you dare tell Hayley about the murder, Abigail Summers."

"As if I would. I'm not that insensitive, Lillian. You know me—others, not self."

"Hmm, yes, I think we all know you. So no talk about a gory murder today."

"Cross my heart and hope to die. Our lips are sealed, aren't they, Betty?"

"She'll be on her best behaviour. I won't let her say a word, dear."

As they rounded the bend of the canal, Terry saw the lady from the adjacent boat stepping onto the rear of Trevor's and knocking. Her husband was just behind her.

"Trevor, are you okay? It's not like you to still be in bed."

"Leave him alone, Rosa. He probably had a skinful at the pub. Or maybe he's got a girl in there."

"I've never seen his curtains pulled this late. He's usually sitting on the back having his second coffee by now. I tell you, it's not like him."

Lillian said, "You go, girl, take no notice of him."

Luckily, Rosa didn't. And after knocking for the third time, she entered. On hearing the scream, her husband followed her in.

"God, Rosa, let's get out. I'll call the police. Don't touch anything."

She took her hands away from her mouth. "Do you think he fell on his pen?"

"And then turned over? Doubt it, woman. Come on. They might think it's us."

"Who would think that?"

"Plenty of people. He always did fancy you, so they might think it's me."

"Rubbish. We were just good friends."

"So you say. Come on. You're dropping your DNA everywhere."

After they had gone, the four ghosts got onboard.

Terry said, "There's quite a bit of alcohol about. Do you think you could have fallen?"

"No. But it could be why the wife kicked me out."

"Let me look at you," said Lillian. "I suppose you could have fallen. But that mark on your face looks like a punch to me. And if your whole weight fell on the pen, it would have gone in a lot further. It's harder than you think to puncture skin. I'm guessing he or she got lucky and caught your heart. There's not much blood, so you died quite quickly."

"That's good to hear," said Trevor.

Suzie sat at the table. "This is your latest book. Well, ideas and notes for it." She pulled some screwed-up paper out of the bin. "This is from your book as well."

"Looks like I was having a bit of writer's block then. If I'm an author, I must have a computer or a laptop. God knows where."

Terry said, "If you were going to the pub, I reckon you would have hidden it. A boat isn't that secure. Try in the drawers, Suzie."

She eventually found it under a cushion, but Terry said, "You'd better leave it. We might muck it up. The police have tech experts. I have no idea how you turn one on."

"Of course, it was slates in your day, wasn't it?" joked Suzie.

"Cheeky monkey. I can hear the sirens, can you? It's a shame Tom won't be here."

"He'll be off for a while. I think they get two weeks off now for paternity leave," said Lillian.

"I'm sure it was never that in my day."

"That's because they kept the mums in for a good week," added Lillian. "And they think it's a good idea for the men to bond with the baby. Which is true. Let's go and see who's here."

It was WPC Jane Nichols and a young police constable they didn't know. But he introduced himself to Rosa and her husband as PC Alex Coult. He put the yellow tape around the barge, and they talked to the couple until Johnson and Mills arrived.

Terry said, "I wonder if our inspector is still in love. We'll soon know by what mood he's in."

A good one, as they soon learned.

"Morning all. There's something romantic about these fancy barges. I used to come here when I was a kid. What happened then, Jane?"

"There's the body of Trevor Grand in that one, sir. He's about fifty, and he's quite a well-known author of murder books."

"Ironic then. If it is a murder."

"This is Del and Rosa Maguire. They live on this one and found the body when they saw the curtains were still drawn." She conveyed what she had been told to her superiors. Mills told PC Coult to look around for any witnesses or anything out of the ordinary.

"No sign of the doctor or forensics?" asked the DCI.

"They're on their way, sir. Shouldn't be long."

"Let's have a quick look then, Dave. Blimey, you can't swing a rat in here."

"At least you can stand up straight, sir."

"Are you calling me short, sonny?"

"No. I'm saying the ceiling is low, sir."

"Very diplomatic. Poor bloke. Looks like he's been punched and then stabbed. What is that?"

"Looks like a fountain pen with the lid on." Mills put on his gloves and touched the body on the arm. "Rigour has set in. Jane was told he went to the pub most nights, so it could be a drunken accident. Looks like he came in, and then it happened. Coat and keys are there. Or maybe he had a fight and was followed back here. I wonder what his local was."

"You've got the Globe that way and the Fishery Inn down there," said Johnson. "It's my superpower; I know all the pubs around here. Let's go and ask the neighbours, they'll know."

"It was the Fishery. I wouldn't say he went every night, but most," said Del.

Johnson asked, "Nice bloke, was he? Any enemies?"

"He was friendly enough. Kept to himself. And was always scribbling away at something for his books. I can't think who would want to hurt him. He had a few female friends come. He was divorced, I think, and had a couple of kids. Trevor wasn't the sort to start a fight at the pub. A nice, gentle sort."

Trevor himself was very glad to hear his kind words.

"Let's have a walk to the Fishery then, Sergeant," said Johnson. "It's our duty to check. Good beer, is it, sir?"

"None better round here."

"Come on then, Dave. Oh, look, it's lunchtime. You can treat me to lunch as well. Jane, you stand guard here until the others arrive."

But Johnson was not going to get his free beer and lunch. Mills' phone went. It was the agitated young constable.

"Calm down, Alex. What's the matter? Don't move, we're coming. We've got another one, sir."

"Another boat?"

"No. Another body."

Chapter 28

THE BODY WAS HIDDEN IN LONG GRASS FURTHER UP the towpath that led towards the Fishery Inn. PC Coult looked very pale as he pointed to a bare foot sticking out.

"It's a woman, sir."

"Oh no," said Mills gravely. "Okay, Alex, go and get the tape and secure the scene. You did well to find her." Mills noticed how quiet his boss was. "Are you all right, sir? You look a bit white."

"I'm fine," said Johnson quietly. "Do we know who she is? Any ID on her?"

"Can't see a bag. I'll check her pockets. Nothing there. Shame. Pretty lady."

The victim had shoulder-length dyed blonde hair, and she was wearing a black top and tight jeans.

"Can you see the cause of death, Mills?"

"Blood coming from a head wound, but none on the body as far as I can see. Or in the surrounding area. Maybe she was brought here after she was dead."

Johnson looked away. "I'll leave you to it, Sergeant. You know what to do. Stay here till the team comes, and get more uniforms doing a search. Let me know when you've identified her."

"Are you walking up to the Fishery, then?"

"No, I'm going back to the station. I'd forgotten I had to do something, and I want to brief the Chief Commissioner in person. You can handle it. Keep me posted," Johnson told him as he walked back to the car.

Terry was the first to say, "Is it me, or was DCI Johnson hiding something? He looked shocked, and I think he knew her. I tell you what, I'm going with him. He's up to something. You three stay here, and we'll meet at the library later."

After Terry had gone, Lillian asked Trevor if he recognised the lady.

"I don't know her, but something has come back to me. I did go to the pub last night. I was walking back, it was dark, but not that dark, and I thought I saw someone fly-tipping again. They're always doing it round here. You'd be surprised what rubbish they throw in the canal or in the hedges. I saw a man carrying something, and then he threw it in the bushes. So I shouted out, 'Oi,' and he punched me on the chin, and I ran. I didn't see him follow me, so I unlocked the door and went in, thinking he'd gone. But he must have been behind me. And I don't want to think about the next bit."

"Can you describe him?"

"That's the annoying thing. He needn't have killed me. Other than him being tall and thinnish, I know nothing. It could be anyone."

"His DNA will be on your face and on the pen, unless he wore gloves," said Lillian. "I wonder how the lady died. If she had been shot or stabbed, he'd have used that weapon on you."

Suzie said, "We do miss Tom and Hayley. We could get going and just get Hayley to find out all the things like names and addresses."

"I know. So we'd better stay and see what the doctor and

forensics find out. We'll let everyone know later. It'll be interesting to see if we can do a whole investigation with no help from the other side."

"I think we'll have to, Lillian. It'll be weeks before Hayley is back to normal."

"Yes, Hayley will have other mysteries to solve now. Like how to change a nappy and how to get a baby to sleep through the night."

But when Abigail and Betty got to the hospital, Benjamin was fast asleep.

"He's the most perfect little thing I've ever seen, Hayley," said Abigail. "Look at those tiny fingers and button nose. And all that hair. He's gorgeous."

"Thanks, hun. We love him to bits already. Though he scares me to death. For goodness' sake, don't wake him. I'd be too frightened to pick him up."

"You needn't worry, they're a lot more robust than they look. They don't actually break, dear," said Betty.

"Did it hurt much?" asked Abigail.

"Like hell."

"She's right, dear. If I'd have had a gun, I would have shot myself. But you soon forget, and then you do it all again."

"No way. That's it now."

"I said that too, before I had the next two. Mind you, John only had to look at me to get me pregnant."

"He didn't just look, from what you tell us," said Abigail. "Where's the proud father?"

"He went home to get changed. We left so quick in the night, he forgot to put his pants and socks on. At least we had everything ready. What good timing from the village to finish the nursery. I was hoping to have a sleep when Tom had gone. Do you mind?"

"We'll go in a minute," said Betty.

"We can't stay too long anyway," said Abigail.

"Why? Has something happened?" asked Hayley excitedly.

Abigail was saved from lying by a nurse walking over to the bed. "Are you all right, Mrs Bennett? I thought I heard talking."

"Er, just to the baby. I'm trying to bond."

"You might do that better if you held him."

"I will in a minute. Thank you." To Abigail and Betty, she said, "You've got me in trouble again. You'll get me locked up one day. But now you've said it, you might as well tell me what's happened."

"Nothing's happened. I swear on my life," said Abigail. "Anyway, Lillian would kill me if I told you. You know I'm not her favourite person at the best of times."

"Come on, Betty, spill."

"Well, I didn't exactly promise myself, and I suppose if you asked me questions, it would be rude not to at least nod."

"Okay," whispered Hayley. "Has there been a murder? Yes. In Becklesfield? Okay, no. It's like charades. Do the police know yet? You don't know. How did you find out without me or Tom knowing? Is the victim still here? I see. Do you want me to tell Tom?"

"Definitely not," snapped Abigail. "We're doing very well. We know who he is, where he lived, we just need to find out who killed him. We've got it all under control. The others are at the canal with the body. Damn, I shouldn't have told you that. I told you nothing if Lillian asks."

"Your secret is safe, and anyway, get going. I need to sleep while the baby does."

Hayley wriggled down the bed, but it was the sign of things to come; as Hayley shut her eyes, Benjamin Michael Bennett opened his and let out a loud cry. Abigail and Betty could hear him all the way down the corridor.

"What an awful noise," said Abigail. "Why does something

that cute have to have such an awful noise come out of it? It goes right through you."

"That's the idea. It's so you can't ignore it and have to stop whatever you're doing and see to it."

"And shut it up. In that case, it works perfectly," said Abigail, putting her hands over her ears.

As the two spirits left the ward, Tom walked in and wondered what that dreadful noise was.

"Where have you been?" shouted Hayley.

"Sorry, love. Mum came round with this teddy, and I sat down and fell asleep. I was knackered."

"Were you?! I'm so pleased you had a little nap."

"I take it that's sarcasm."

"You could say that. It must have been very tiring to watch me push your huge son out in total agony."

"I'm sorry, darling. I'll hold him, and you have a sleep."

"Oh, I'm sorry too, hun. I don't know why I'm so snappy. It's supposed to be the happiest day of our lives, isn't it? Hopefully, they say I can go home tomorrow. What if he cries like that at home? Oh, what have we done, Tom? I've no idea what to do with a baby. Nor have you."

"Mum said she'll come over as soon as we get back. And your parents can't wait to come."

"Did you phone work and tell them?"

"Yes, they all said congratulations and to send their best to you. I rang Jane and then Dave. He was… actually, that doesn't matter."

"He was what?"

"It's nothing, just work. Shall I get Benjie out?"

"Don't change the subject. He's gone back to sleep anyway. They've found a body, haven't they? Don't forget I'm a psychic."

"Not that psychic, they found two bodies."

"Really? I'm seeing water and a boat."

Tom looked surprised. "You are good. It was at the Grand

Union Canal. A man was found on a barge, and a woman was found not that far away on the towpath. And I love it, because this time you-know-who can't get you involved. And you won't be able to tell your ghostly buddies about it. They'll be mad when they find out," laughed Tom.

"They sure will, hun. I promise I won't tell them. Now let me have a sleep while he's quiet, for goodness' sake."

The same nurse as before came over. "Good news, Hayley, you can go home. We need to get the paperwork done and check baby over, and then you can go."

"Are you sure? It seems a bit soon."

"Benjamin is perfectly fine."

"I'm talking about me. I feel like I've been run over by a truck."

"All new mothers feel like that. You'll feel much better when you get back home. It should be about half an hour," said the nurse as she hurried off.

"Well, that's it then," said Hayley. "God help us."

"We'll be fine. Mum can come, and you can have a sleep."

"You're forgetting I have to feed him. If I can. Talk about being thrown to the wolves."

"Don't exaggerate. More like thrown to the cat. Luna wonders what on earth is going on. I'll start packing up, then I'll have to go and get the baby seat out of the car. It took me half an hour to put it in. How I'll do it with a baby in, I have no idea."

"See, everything is a challenge. But I suppose we'll laugh about this one day. And millions of others manage to do it, so how hard can it be? You might as well tell me a bit more about the case while I get changed."

"Not a lot to tell. The doctor is there now, so I don't know everything. The man is Trevor Grand, the mystery writer. He was stabbed with his own fountain pen on his barge. Another boat owner found him. They haven't identified the woman yet.

Apparently, my replacement, Alex Coult, looks a bit green. It's his first murder."

"Perhaps one saw the other one murdered. The woman could have been running away."

"Hayley, you're not supposed to be doing your sleuthing. That's it, I'm not telling you any more about the bodies. But I have got some other news about Johnson."

"Ooh, tell me, hun."

"When he saw the dead woman, he went white as a sheet, made an excuse, and left pronto."

"It's not like him to be so sensitive. Usually, he asks who has ruined his day by getting themselves killed, so he must know her. But why didn't he say he knew her? I hope it wasn't the one he'd been seeing."

"Don't even go there. We're supposed to be having a break, remember, Hayley? I've got two glorious weeks off with no robberies or murders. Just me and you and little Benjamin."

Chapter 29

TERRY HAD JUMPED INTO JOHNSON'S CAR JUST BEFORE he drove off and was surprised when he pulled into a lay-by after five minutes. He grabbed the steering wheel with both hands and hit his forehead on it three times. Terry heard mumbling that contained every swear word he knew, followed by Johnson blowing out his cheeks, which seemed to settle him down, and he drove on.

They were on the way back to Gorebridge—Terry assumed to the police station—but then the inspector turned left at some traffic lights and stopped outside a smart-looking block of flats. But as if he suddenly thought of something, he restarted the engine, drove around the corner, and walked back. Terry wondered if it was where he lived, but they looked out of his price range. Although he knew Johnson wouldn't be averse to taking a bribe or two.

After opening the outside door with a key, Terry followed him up the stairs to flat number 8, Banbury Court. Once inside, Johnson worked quickly. He grabbed a towel and started wiping fingerprints off anything he thought he might have touched over the last few months. He knew the drill and tried to think what sort of thing forensics would dust. He was keeping as quiet as he could. The nosy woman across the hall had eyes like a hawk and ears like a nosy bat. Her husband was as bad.

"Where have I been?" Johnson said to himself. Definitely the bathroom and bedroom. The kitchen, not so much, but he would do it anyway. He got out his crime scene gloves and was annoyed at himself for not thinking of them sooner. He made for the side of the bed he slept on and wiped the headboard as he remembered happy times. He stopped and looked at the large photograph of Angie when she was a young model. How beautiful she was then. He had been a lucky man, but not anymore. TV remote—yes, they'd watched a film together last weekend: Die Hard. The thought made him sad, and he pursed his lips and got on.

"Where's her phone?" It wasn't on the body. That was strange. She never went anywhere without her big handbag either.

Then he looked for anything of his. There was a jumper on one of the armchairs, and he saw a bottle of whisky that he had definitely touched, deciding to take it with him. He needed a drink. But where was the empty bottle of the cheap champagne they'd shared the other night? The one he had bought when they decided on a day to get married. He had never been so happy. Hopefully, Angie had got rid of it in the bin and the dustman had taken it away.

He went into the kitchen to wipe the work surfaces, and that was when he saw the blood up the walls and cupboards and the pool of blood on the floor.

He sat down on a chair and put his hands on his head. "Angie, I'm so sorry. I'll get him. And I don't mean arrest. I'll get him, that I promise."

Johnson had a last look around the flat and left, remembering to wipe what he had touched as he'd come in. Terry stayed with him until he got back to the station, then made his way back to Becklesfield by bus. Boy, had he learned a lot. He had the first name and address of the second victim. He wished he could let Tom know because he didn't think Johnson would be telling anyone. And he couldn't wait to tell Abigail—she'd know what to do.

Unfortunately, Abigail wasn't back from the hospital, so he waited with the others till she came back with Betty. The library had closed for the day, so they didn't have to worry about causing chills or attracting the attention of any small children.

Abigail took charge as usual when she walked in. "Before we start, Betty and I saw baby Benjie, and he is gorgeous and Hayley is doing fine. We timed it well—Tom had popped home."

"He is a little angel," said Betty.

"But he sounds like the very devil. Imagine a deranged duck that is getting strangled—that's the only way of explaining it."

"You haven't had a lot of experience with babies, have you?" said Terry.

"Not up close, and I'm beginning to realise why."

"You didn't tell her about the murders, did you, Abigail?" asked Lillian.

"I didn't say a word, on your life."

Betty had to admit, "She did guess, though. Don't forget she's a psychic. She took it right out of my mind that a man had been found dead on a boat, but that's it. I only answered a few of her questions. I had to be truthful, dear."

"I forgot about her being psychic. Okay, Betty, never mind. But what you couldn't tell her is that a new PC found another body." Lillian told Abigail and Betty all that she knew. Then Terry had his turn.

"We were right—she was Johnson's fancy woman. And listen to this, he drove straight to her flat in Gorebridge and wiped his fingerprints off everything."

The Deadly Wedding

"Why would he do that if he hadn't done anything wrong?" said Suzie.

"Exactly. Mind you, he seemed really brokenhearted about it, so it wasn't that he killed her." Terry told them what else he saw in the flat.

Lillian recounted how Trevor had remembered that it was a tall man that he saw throwing the body in the hedgerow like a bag of rubbish, so it couldn't be Johnson.

"And she didn't have any ID on her, and it was a woman doctor this time. She said the victim had received blunt force trauma to the head but didn't know if that had killed her yet. And she had most likely been killed somewhere else and taken there. But we already knew that. She could only guess at the time of death but thought it was sometime yesterday afternoon or evening. Mills made a good point—he said she must have been dumped after dark, as the foot was sticking out and someone would have noticed it in the daytime."

Trevor said, "And the doctor thought I was killed between eleven and one in the morning. The only thing she got wrong was that she said I'd been punched and then stabbed together. But I was punched a bit before that. Not that it matters, I suppose. Can't we just tell your friend who the lady is to hurry things up a bit?"

Abigail shook her head. "No, we can do this on our own. They'll probably work it out soon by fingerprints, or someone will have called missing persons. Tom would be mad if we involved her so soon after having the baby. She might even be home later today. We need to have more faith in Sergeant Mills."

Suzie said, "Why don't me, Lillian, and Terry go and have a proper snoop at the flat tomorrow? He might be there as well, and we can see what they've found out. What are you going to do, Abigail?"

"I think now we know the victims, we should try and find some suspects. I'm going to see Celia at the Chiltern Weekly—

she should be able to help. You should come with us, Trevor. Celia Hanson is a well-known journalist with an eidetic memory. She worked for the paper as a crime reporter."

"Sounds good. Is she psychic?"

"No, she's dead."

"Even so, I'd love to go with you, Abigail," smiled Trevor. "It will be like a date." Abigail noticed for the first time what a lovely smile he had under that beard.

But Terry had other ideas. "Oi, she's my bird."

"What are you, a hundred years old?" Trevor said sarcastically.

"Give or take, yes. We've been courting for months now. Tell him, Abi."

"It's true, but I'm beginning to regret it when you refer to me as a bird that belongs to you."

"Well, you know what I mean. I'm just saying."

"I'm sorry," said Trevor. "I had no idea. I'll keep away."

"You'll do no such thing," snapped Abigail. "You're coming to Gorebridge to see Celia, and that's that. But I was going to say Betty is coming before you get all heated, Terry. I never knew you were the jealous type."

"Me? No way."

"It's just work, Terry. I think it's very strange that Johnson went to all that trouble for nothing. If someone is trying to frame him, it could be from one of his old cases. Let's face it, he could have easily put away an innocent man. Or, once or twice, even a guilty one. So it could take a while."

"Well, we've got all the time in the world," said Trevor, with a smug look at Terry, which he didn't like at all.

Chapter 30

AT THE HOUSE IN CHURCH LANE, IT WAS JUST BEFORE six o'clock the following morning, and Benjamin had woken up every two hours. Hayley had given up and gone downstairs to have a cup of camomile tea. Luna quite liked this new thing that woke them up. Maybe he would get his first breakfast this early every day. When he first saw the bundle, he walked towards it, but it moved, so he backed away. And with all that noise, Luna hoped it would be gone in a few days.

After feeding the cat to stop him meowing so loudly, Hayley took her tea into the sitting room and turned the television on, but then quickly turned the volume down. She had been so busy that she hadn't had the time or the strength to put on her phone to see what was happening in the world.

The weatherman said it was going to be a cold but sunny day. That was good at least. If she had time to do some washing, maybe Tom's mum could put it out on the line. Her attention was caught by the first news report.

"In the double murder at the Grand Union Canal at Little Frimble, two bodies have been found and identified as forty-eight-year-old Angie Metcalfe of Gorebridge and the thriller writer, Trevor Grand. It is not yet known how the deaths are connected. Gorebridge Police are not giving any more information at this time," said the newsreader.

"Well, well, well, Luna. I wonder if Abigail knows yet. Gone are the days when I can just run to the library and tell her. For now, anyway. Tom will be back at work in a couple of weeks, and then things will get back to normal. They drive me up the wall coming in and out, but now I really miss them all. I bet you do too." Hayley tickled Luna's neck but then heard a voice say her name, which made her jump and Luna leap off her lap.

"Hayley, darling."

"Nanny, you came."

"Of course I did," said a small white-haired lady with pink cheeks. "You don't think I'd miss seeing my first great-grandchild just because I'm not alive anymore, do you? He's beautiful, Hayley, like his mum. He's got the gift, I can tell."

"I think so too, Nan."

"You'll be there for him. Like I was for you. You look tired, dear. You must sleep when he sleeps."

"If he ever does for more than five minutes, I'll try. By the time I've finished feeding and changing him, he's awake again. I'll give it another day or two, and then I'll get Tom to go to the chemist and get some bottles."

"Whatever is best for you. That's why they sell it. Your baby, your rules. Do you still use your gift?"

"I do. I make a bit of money from it as Hayley Moon. And I help the police when I can."

"Well done. I wish I could have done that. I always felt I wasted what God had given me. I'm so proud of you."

"Can you stay? Please, I need you. I'm scared to death of being a mum. I don't know if I can do it. I've stood in front of murderers and been less scared than I am of carrying Benjie and putting his clothes on him. And they expect me to give him a bath, and he'll be as slippery as a wet frog. I literally can't do it, Nan."

"Babies are a lot more robust than they look. For what it's worth, I can see Benjie well into the future. You and your little family are going to be just fine, Hayley."

"I know, but don't go, Nan, please."

"I have to, sweetheart. But I'll come back. Remember, I love you."

Hayley felt a cold kiss on her cheek and closed her eyes. When she opened them, she was on her own and wondered if she had dreamed it all. But the fact that Luna was hiding under the sofa and shaking was enough to convince her that she hadn't.

Even when she heard Benjamin crying half an hour later, she still had a smile on her face, and she felt for the first time that she could cope.

Chapter 31

THE WORST THING ABOUT HAYLEY BEING OUT OF action was that they had to catch a bus. So that morning, they caught the nine o'clock bus from outside the Post Office to Gorebridge. Terry, Lillian, and Suzie got off first and walked to the victim's flat in Banbury Court. They could see right away that she had been identified, as Jane Nichols and Alex Coult were standing outside and talking to the locals who wanted to know what was going on. As they were listening to what was being said, Sergeant Mills arrived.

"Morning, sir."

"Morning, Jane."

"No DCI Johnson today?" she said hopefully.

"No. He's got something personal to do. I'll brief him later."

While the police were chatting, Terry said, "That is very unusual for Johnson."

"But he can't come. The neighbours would recognise him, probably," said Lillian.

They followed Mills upstairs, where he met Bob from forensics leaving.

"All done, Dave. There's not a lot of fingerprints. It's like someone went round and wiped the places a visitor would have touched." A colleague walked by with a plastic container of sealed bags. "We found a few things, though. A toothbrush and two glasses and plates that were in the dishwasher. Might get prints off them, or DNA."

"What about a murder weapon?"

"You're not that lucky, I'm afraid. You'll see the blood spatter in the kitchen. We've got plenty of photos and samples."

"Thanks, Bob. Ring me when you get any results."

"No DCI today?"

"No. Don't ask."

"I won't, but it's nice, isn't it? Bye, Dave."

Mills called to Jane to come and help him with the search. "What are we looking for, sir?"

"Anything that shows who was with her when she was killed. That would be the day before yesterday, Sunday. We know it was done in the kitchen, so be careful where you stand. In fact, I'll go in there. You start here. Good, you've got your gloves on."

"There's a lovely photo of her in here, sir. I reckon she might have been a model when she was young," Jane shouted from the bedroom.

Suzie watched as she went through all the drawers and the fitted wardrobe. She didn't see any men's clothes, and in the bathroom, there were no signs of a man having shaved there. But all it took was for him to have been there once, two days ago. The spirits heard Mills say he was going into the kitchen, so they joined him, and Jane stood by the door.

"What do you reckon, Jane? Looks to me like she was making a coffee with her back to her assailant."

"Yes, coffee granules over the floor. And only one cup there, so she probably wasn't making her visitor one. Perhaps she didn't know him, or know he was there. So he must have broken in."

"Very good. You spotted that before me. Blood spatter on the upper cupboard mostly, so I reckon you're right. And a pool on the floor. When he carried her out, he must have got blood on his clothes and shoes. There's no sign of her being dragged. Once we get a suspect, we can get him on that. As long as he or she hasn't got rid of them."

"What do you know about her, sir?"

"She was forty-eight. Single, but not divorced. She'd gone back to her maiden name, so we need to check more. It's early days. We have no idea if she worked, but we will. We need to find the ex as soon as we can. And no signs it was a burglary. The TV is still here, and no signs of anyone rifling through her stuff."

"No other suspects?"

"Not yet. Let's go and talk to the neighbours. They might know. You check the flats below, I'll do this floor, numbers six and seven."

Jane was enjoying today. Not only was the sexist DCI Johnson off, but so was Tom Bennett, and she was doing what he usually did—question witnesses.

Mills took off his gloves and knocked at the door of 6, Banbury Court. A smartly dressed, plump, middle-aged woman answered the door within seconds. Mills thought she must be the sort to enjoy such a thing happening on her doorstep.

"Come on in, Inspector."

"Sergeant Mills, actually. Could I ask some questions about your neighbour, Angie Metcalfe? I assume you heard she was murdered."

"I saw it on the television earlier. They didn't say much, though, apart from calling it the canal murders. How was she killed?"

"I can't tell you any more at present."

"Please sit down. Howard, the police are here! They want to know about Angie. There's a lot to tell, believe me. Hurry up, Howard. Do sit down; the police haven't got all day."

Mills nodded to the man as he joined them. He looked every inch the henpecked husband.

Mills got out his pad and pen and took their names: Howard and Hilda Waterman.

"How well did you know her?" He guessed that she would answer first.

"I wouldn't say we were friends. The only time we talked was when we met in the hall."

"Did she work, do you know?"

"Not that one. Probably never worked a day in her life, wasn't that right, Howard? She always had plenty of money, though. I used to wonder if she was, you know."

"No, I don't know, Mrs Waterman."

"I'm not saying she was, Sergeant, but she always had a lot of gentlemen friends. She was the typical brassy blonde."

"That's not true, er, dear. And I happen to know she was a natural blonde."

They both looked at Howard in surprise. "I saw a photo of her. She used to be a model. There were a few men, but lately, it was just one in particular."

"She could wrap men around her little finger, that one. But as Howard says, there was a new one that had been on the scene for a few months. A scruffy, common little man. Always stank of whisky. And he had the cheek to leave his car right outside so we couldn't park in front of our own home," Hilda said. "If you ask me, he was too drunk to drive and left it here overnight. I'd see a taxi pull up sometimes."

"I don't suppose you know the name of the taxi firm?"

"Stars Cars. I was coming home one night, and he was getting in. I heard him tell the driver where he lives. Some flats, I think, I can't remember now. The odd night he'd stay here with her."

"Any other visitors, like other women?"

"I suppose one or two occasionally. But I think she preferred the company of men, don't you, Howard?"

"If you say so, Hilda. I don't know."

"We think she was murdered two days ago, so Sunday afternoon or early evening. Were you at home?"

"Sunday, we usually go to our daughter's for dinner and always get back about nine o'clock, so no. What a shame. It's typical, the most exciting thing that's happened for years," she added.

"How long had she lived here?"

"About two years, wasn't it, Howard? I seem to remember she left her husband. Not a nice man by all accounts."

"I don't suppose you know her latest male visitor's name, do you, Mrs Waterman?"

"I'm sorry, no. But you might be able to find him by his car. I know the number plate begins with BRK."

"And the make and colour?"

"Now that I do know. It was a dark blue Toyota. And it had a large dent on the passenger's door."

Mills suddenly had a bad feeling. He knew someone with a Toyota with a dent on the passenger door. And his number plate began with BRK. He always remembered it as it reminded him of the word berk, and how appropriate it was. So things began to fall into place.

Terry and the others saw the look on Mills' face and were sure he had realised the lady was talking about Johnson.

"I think that'll be all for now. But we might need to speak to you again. Will your neighbour at number seven be there?"

"Sean White? Yes, he'll be in. He works nights at the plastic factory as a night watchman. He's usually asleep by now, but he wouldn't be missing all this excitement. And he had a soft spot for her next door. Always offering to take her parcels in. But she always said no. We did that for her. She wouldn't look twice at him. Not exactly God's gift, if you know what I mean."

"Thank you very much. If you think of anything else, please ring the station."

Mills, and even the ghosts, were very pleased to get out of there. Mrs Waterman was not a nice person.

The man who answered the door on their next call was a tall, thin man who was in his dressing gown. Like the woman had said, he wasn't likely to attract the likes of his neighbour. But then Johnson was no oil painting either, thought Lillian.

"I suppose you'd better come in. I don't know anything though, so you're wasting your time."

"I'm Sergeant Mills. Could I have your name, please, sir?"

"Sean White. But everyone calls me Chalky. Sit down. Can I get you a cup of tea?"

Mills would have loved one, but he just wanted to get this last statement and find Johnson. If he hadn't left the country.

"Could you turn the television off, please? Were you here on Sunday, Mr White? In the afternoon and evening?"

"I went to the local for a lunchtime pint and got back at about four."

"How well did you know Angie? Not as well as you would have liked to, I heard."

"I bet I know who told you that. I'd take everything she says with a pinch of salt. Stirrer, that's what she is. And jealous of Angie. We'd chat if we met, that was about it."

"Did you see anyone hanging around when you got back on Sunday, or hear any noise from next door?"

"No and no. I live on my own. And to kill the hours, I always have my television on. Probably louder than I should. I don't like my own company, and I hate the quiet. Are you married, Sergeant?"

"Yes, sir." He didn't want to ask about Johnson, but he had to. "Your neighbour said a man had been a regular visitor to Mrs Metcalfe lately."

"Huh, I know the one. Scruffy little beggar. Well, you'd know. Can't be him though. He's one of your lot—a policeman."

"How do you know that, sir?"

"I told you, I like my telly on. I've seen him on there giving news conferences. I think his name is Inspector Johnson."

Chapter 32

ABIGAIL AND BETTY LUCKILY FOUND CELIA HANSON IN the editor's office. Trevor said he had something to do first and that he would catch up with them later. Celia was there most days since she had died. She had loved her job on the paper and had been their chief reporter for deaths, inquests, and crime—mostly the murders. With her photographic memory, she could spot any link between cases, and she saved The Deadly Detective Agency many hours of scrolling through the library files at night to look at cold cases.

The only thing Abigail didn't like about her was that, even in death, she was dressed and made up immaculately; her bobbed hair was shiny and perfect. Whereas Abigail had died in bed and always felt like the poor sister, complete with bed hair at the back.

Celia's first words were, "Don't tell me, you've come about the Canal Murders."

"How did you guess? Is there any more news?" asked Abigail.

"They know the woman is Angie Metcalfe now, and they've got her address. And he's the author, Trevor Grand."

"We'd worked that out. Shall we find somewhere a bit more private?" said Abigail, looking at the editor, Oliver, who was talking on the phone and getting on Abigail's nerves. The three of them walked back down to the reception area and found some chairs in a private corner.

"So, tell me all about it," said Celia excitedly.

"We haven't got any suspects..."

"Not about the murders, silly. I want to hear about the baby."

Abigail sighed impatiently, so Betty said, "Benjamin is gorgeous. You'll have to come and see him. Hayley's doing well, but she's shattered. And we've been very good at giving her some space. It's not been easy finding things out without her. And Tom's no help because he's off on paternity leave."

"Actually, we've known more than the police have, so it works both ways. We knew she was Angie and where she lived within the hour. And there's something else we know that they don't—she was the girlfriend of DCI Johnson!" said Abigail proudly.

"No? I heard he was seeing someone. Do you think that's why she was killed? Or did he do it?"

"We don't know anything about her yet. Could be another lover, for all we know. But Johnson went to her flat after the murder and wiped his prints and took his stuff; Terry was following him. And we know he didn't kill her because he was devastated. And another thing that will shock you—we have a witness who saw her body being dumped, and it wasn't the inspector. It was a much taller and thinner man."

"And the police don't know? He'll have to go and tell them."

"He'll have a job. It's Trevor Grand, the other victim!"

"And he's got the hots for Abigail. Terry was as green as a beetroot," giggled Betty.

"Red," corrected Celia.

"No, he was definitely green. Anyway, Terry was very jealous.

He really didn't want Trevor to come with us today. He'll be here in a minute, dear. He is rather dishy."

"He is quite good-looking, Celia," said Abigail. "But Terry's got nothing to worry about. We're such good friends—that's why I love him so much. And he knows all my ways and still loves me."

"That's not Trevor Grand, is it? That gorgeous bloke with the beard, in the checked shirt that's just come in?"

Betty smiled. "Yes, that's Trevor."

But then it was Abigail's turn to be jealous. The writer made a beeline for Celia and held his hand out.

"Hello. You must be Celia. They never told me you were so beautiful. You and I have a lot in common—both writers."

"I see you come with your own pen," said Celia tersely, bringing him back to reality. She wasn't going to be flattered by all that beautiful talk. Minds were more important to her.

"Yes, it's very unfortunate, but a good reminder that I'm dead. I've just been to the bookshop to look at my books. I saw about five of mine there. I feel quite sad that I won't be able to write anymore. But, in a way, it's kind of a relief. At least there are no more deadlines."

"I miss the deadlines of the newspaper. It was my life. I put it before my personal life and never had time for relationships or having children. Not that I wanted them."

"I have two children, but I have no idea where they are."

"The paper is looking into you, so I'm sure I'll be able to tell you. I don't miss much here," said Celia.

"Or our agency can find out for you, dear. All problems great and small is our motto, isn't it, Abigail?"

"If we get time," she snapped. Trevor and Celia were getting on far too well for her liking. "Let's find out who killed you first. We were wondering if Angie could have been murdered to punish Tony Johnson, Celia. Or if they're trying to frame him, even. It's the only place we can start for now. So, knowing how brilliant your memory is, do you remember anyone that he put away, and who has been released in the last month or so?"

"You don't want much, Abigail. Assuming they didn't serve their full sentence, you expect me to think of someone who was, say, sentenced to ten years and released or paroled after five—with no name."

"I suppose we could rule out murderers."

"Not necessarily. Let me think." Celia looked up and shut her eyes.

"Anything?" said Abigail impatiently.

"Give me a minute. Um. There was one bloke. I hadn't been working here long then. It was one of my first court coverages. He threatened Johnson as he was dragged out of court. His exact words were, 'I'm going to get your family, as long as it takes. You'd better watch your back.' I always remember because the whole jury laughed when Tony said, 'I've just got two ex-wives, so go for it.'"

Trevor said, "You really are amazing, Celia. Can you remember his name?"

"Please, I remember everything. Brydon Hurst. July 2017. Ten years for grievous bodily harm. Sentenced to ten years. He beat a bloke in the pub half to death who criticised his wife. She left him and went into hiding before the trial ended, taking his kids. Hurst blamed Johnson, not his own temper. But I've no idea if he's out yet."

"We'll have to pass that on somehow. Is there anyone recently that he could have upset? Maybe put them away. This year, perhaps?"

"His latest arrest was for the Wedding Murders. But George Arnold is safely locked up. And I can't see anyone wanting to help him. Um… there's the Newsome case," Celia recalled.

"That rings a bell," said Abigail.

"It should do. You knew one of the victims. She and her husband were shot in the back."

"Of course." Abigail turned to Trevor. "It was last year. Terry and I were walking to Halton Thorpe to get the train to the seaside, and a lady called my name and said she was off on a cruise to South America, and she wanted some outfits altered. We had to tell her that she wouldn't be going on a cruise as she'd been shot in the back."

"That's right," said Betty. "You brought her back to the library, and we told Hayley, who told Tom. She said the last person she saw was a chap from Gorebridge, and he'd been shouting at her husband."

Celia said, "That's it. You didn't get the credit—Johnson did. Once he had the name and found the bodies at their house, stuffed under the wooden decking in the garden in black bags, he arrested him and his thug of a friend."

"They were sentenced to life in January. What was his name? I've forgotten," asked Abigail.

"Martin Reagan. Or Razor Reagan to his enemies and friends." Celia added to Trevor, "Paul Newsome was an accountant and thought he had a brilliant plan to take a cut of Reagan's business on a monthly basis. The money came from drugs, extortion, and women—you know the kind of thing. Newsome said he was taking his wife on a cruise for their ruby wedding anniversary, but really, he had moved the money to an account in Brazil. Reagan didn't get to the top by being naive, and he soon worked it out."

"But surely Reagan and the other man are still in prison. It couldn't be them," said Abigail.

"He's got two brothers. They aren't very nice either, as you can imagine. Reagan thought Johnson was in the pay of a rival gang and stitched him up. He couldn't understand how he caught him so quickly. They found the bodies, and ballistics matched the gun they found at his home within six hours."

"Oh dear," said Abigail, "I feel a bit guilty now if it is

Reagan. They might not even have found the bodies if it wasn't for me."

"That's why Reagan thought Johnson had got inside information. The tickets and suitcases were under the decking with them. The neighbours and friends would have thought they had gone on their romantic cruise a few days later, and nobody would have known they were dead."

"And I would still be alive if Reagan didn't want to frame Johnson," said Trevor. "Thanks for nothing, Abigail. You got me murdered."

"We don't even know it was him yet. You can't blame me." She had gone right off him now. She wished Terry was with her. He would have taken her side. No way would he let someone have a go at her. He might from time to time, but no one else could.

Celia closed her eyes again. "Now, I don't usually believe in coincidences, but can you guess the name of Reagan's estranged wife?"

"You'll have to give us a clue," said Abigail.

"She's dead."

"Angie?!"

Chapter 33

WHILE ALL THE EXCITEMENT WAS GOING ON IN Gorebridge, Tom and Hayley looked at each other as someone knocked at the door. They both needed showers, and the house was a complete mess. Hayley looked through the front window and saw a dark blue car. She heard another knock and couldn't believe that Tony Johnson stood there with a large teddy bear in his arms.

"Hello, sir."

"No need for 'sir' today, Tom. I'm just here as your friend and colleague." Hayley couldn't believe that either.

"Come in, Inspector," she told him.

"Tony, Hayley. Is it convenient? I don't want to intrude. I just wanted to check that my best constable and his wife were all right. And to see how your bonnie daughter is."

"It's a boy," said Hayley, frowning.

"Of course. I knew that."

"Tony, thank you very much for Benjie's present, but I don't think that's why you're really here."

"Ah, maybe you are psychic."

"It's about the canal murders, isn't it? You knew her, I'm guessing. You loved her, more than likely. Have a seat."

"How the hell do you know that? But you're right. I did love Angie. More than I ever have anyone. Can't believe she's gone. She'd agreed to marry me, and I was going to tell everyone. So it wasn't me, Hayley. If it all goes wrong, could you help me? I know I've treated you badly in the past, and you, Tom. But I think I'm being set up to take the fall. And I know who's doing it. Tom, have you heard of Martin Reagan?"

"Razor Reagan? Of course I have."

"I haven't," said Hayley. "I take it he's not good news."

Tom said, "Let's just say he puts the gore in Gorebridge. Nasty bit of work. He's in jail, though, isn't he?"

"Yes, and I put him there. For the Newsome killings. He would only have to get the word out to his brothers or mates. But it's not just that—Angie used to be married to him. She left him a couple of years ago, well before I knew her. But he still didn't like anyone going near her. Reagan married her for her looks, and when they started to fade, he got a younger one, and she was out. Angie didn't mind—she was glad to be shot of him. Luckily, they never had kids. Angie was on the pill without him knowing. She didn't want him anywhere near children. She'd tried to leave him many times but was too frightened to. She'd tried once, and he found her."

"Poor woman. But you think it was him because he found out you were seeing her?"

"That's the only thing I can think of. We started seeing each other after he was arrested. We questioned her—you might remember, Tom."

"I think I do. She lived in a flat."

"That's right. After I saw her body, I went and wiped all my prints off everything. For two reasons: one was that I wanted a bit of time to think about what was happening, and two, if

Reagan didn't know I was seeing her, I didn't want him finding out. He knows a lot of nasty people."

"Do you think it's one of those that killed her and moved the body?" said Hayley.

"I don't know, love. I really don't."

"But they haven't got anything on you. You should have just told Dave Mills the truth when you found the body. You can't get arrested for being her boyfriend."

"I was more than that," he said sadly. "I'll kill the ba—sorry, Hayley. I'll kill whoever did it, I can promise you that."

"Don't worry, Tony," said Hayley. "It could be worse. Well, not much. But I'm sure we'll be able to find out. I believe you, and others will too."

Tom's phone rang, and he excused himself and went to answer it. It was Mills. He had a lot to say about their boss and a murdered woman. So when Tom told him he was with him, Mills said he'd be straight there.

"That was Dave. He's coming round. He didn't say why, but I think he might know your connection to the lady."

"He's a good copper. I trained him too well."

Hayley went and made some tea for everyone. She couldn't believe that Johnson had asked for her help. After all the times he had talked down to her, she was inclined to tell him to get stuffed. But she had her gift for a reason, and there was no getting away from that. Dave knocked just as she was carrying in the tray.

He wasn't his usual cheerful self and barely acknowledged Hayley. She would have gone up to check on Benjie, but she had a feeling something big was going to happen. And for once, he was having a good sleep.

"Out with it then, Dave. What have you found out?" asked Johnson.

"More than I'd like to know, if I'm honest. One of the neighbours gave a description of a man visiting the deceased lady from the canal in her flat lately that sounds a lot like you."

"But that—"

"I haven't finished yet, sir. The description of the car fits, and the taxi firm you used says they took a man from there to your place a couple of times a week."

"Yes, but—"

"And although someone had wiped their prints off, they've got a toothbrush and glasses out of the dishwasher that I'm guessing have your prints and DNA on."

"Ah, that's a bit different. Damn. But as I was just saying, Angie was married to a nasty piece of work. I didn't want him to find out I had anything to do with her. Martin Reagan."

"Razor Reagan? Are you mad?"

"Madly in love, that's all. Anyway, I didn't kill her, and you'll never find the evidence that I did."

"You'll have to come in and give a statement, sir. Leave out the bit about wiping all the prints off—that makes you look guilty. You can say you were so upset you didn't know what you were doing and went home. It's not every day you find your girlfriend's body, and for some reason, I believe you. You might get told off by the Chief Constable, but that's all. That is, unless Mrs Metcalfe finished the relationship and you lost your temper. Then you could have lashed out and tried to cover it up. We've only got your word for it."

"On my old mum's grave. It wasn't me, son."

Hayley said, "I believe him, Dave."

"Okay. Before we go, let's just check your car. We can discount you from our enquiries then. She got to the canal somehow. Tom, can you come and be a witness?"

"You'll find nothing in there, lad. You have my word."

"I know, but we'll just have a quick look. Give me your keys."

The three men went outside to the blue Toyota, where Tom

The Deadly Wedding

and Dave put on their gloves. Hayley watched as Dave lifted the boot, then he took something out. It looked like a handbag, and he put it back before lifting out what looked like a bottle.

Johnson took a step back, and Hayley saw Dave's lips moving. She gasped as she saw him handcuff his shell-shocked boss. As he was led to the other car, Tony shouted out to Hayley, "I didn't do it."

She ran to the door as Tom walked in.

"What the hell just happened?"

"You won't believe it. There was a bag in there, and blood, and something that could have been the murder weapon—an empty champagne bottle. And, I hate to say it, a woman's shoe. He's either being framed, or he's being very clever and putting on a good show."

"I'm sorry, Tom, he's not that clever. He asked for our help, and whether we like him or not, we need to give it to him. I might need you to watch Benjie tomorrow. I've got to get the agency back together."

Chapter 34

It worked out well for Hayley the next day, as Tom's mum had said she couldn't come round, so Hayley left the baby with her husband for the first time to go to the library and get the others to come round. That was one thing Tom couldn't do—unless he went in there and shouted out like a madman that if there was anybody there, they should go with him.

But Hayley was lucky—Terry was walking up the road as she left her house. It was the first time she had been out, and she was still feeling the effects of being in labour for hours. Not only that, she didn't want to look like a bad mother for leaving her baby so soon.

Hayley was all organised when the ghosts arrived; she had fed the baby, and Tom had taken him upstairs to change his nappy. He was very good at that. Luna stayed downstairs—that thing smelled awful. He was getting rather fond of the little thing, though. He had even rubbed his head on his head and tapped him gently on his arm. He was glad to see those other people arrive, who didn't even have to use doors. He had missed them. And he was extra pleased to see his mother, Tiggy. He wanted her to meet the funny little human they had brought home. So, after walking around their legs, Luna and the ginger cat went back up to where the man of the house was. Hopefully, that thing was back in its box.

"This feels like the old days," said Betty as she sat down.

"It's only been just over a week," said Hayley.

"Really? It seems much longer than that. Lillian and Suzie send their apologies, but they've gone to see her friends at the school to check they're all right."

"How's my little grandson? I'm the only one who hasn't met him yet," said Terry.

"He's fine. As soon as we've finished the meeting, we'll go up and you can see him. But I've got so much to tell you all first. About Johnson."

"We know, Hayley," said Abigail smugly. "See, we can do it on our own. He was going out with Martin Reagan's ex-wife."

"Raisin Reagan, as he's known in the gangland," said Betty.

Hayley said excitedly, "Not just that. Don't you know what happened yesterday?"

Abigail said, "Mills found out that Johnson had wiped his prints off in the flat."

"That's old news," said Hayley. She was enjoying knowing something that Abigail didn't. "Johnson actually came here yesterday and asked for our help. But not just that—Dave Mills came round a bit later and said he needed to write a statement, but first, he wanted to check his car to rule him out. And you can guess what happened."

Betty said, "No, I can't."

"When they looked in the boot, they found the murder weapon, which was a champagne bottle, one shoe, and Angie's bag. Oh, and blood. They think he put her in there and took her to the canal!"

"I can't believe it," said Abigail. "Someone must have put them in there."

"Apparently, it didn't look like they had just been placed there. Tom said there were smears of blood and hair as if she had really been in there."

"What about if Angie had finished with him? I bet he's got a temper," said Terry.

"We thought that. So they had to arrest him. I don't know if they will charge him, but it doesn't look good. Fill me in on everything you've found out," said Hayley.

Terry and Lillian recounted what Angie's flat was like and exactly what the neighbours, Hilda and Howard Waterman and Sean White, had said. Then Abigail told her about their visit to Celia at the newspaper.

"So, who was the other suspect Celia told you about, Abigail? Oh, I just thought—where's Trevor?"

"He stayed in Gorebridge. Good riddance, I say," said Abigail.

"Turns out he liked Celia more," said Betty.

"It wasn't just that," Abigail said huffily. "Celia said she'd find out where his children are. And he upset me—more or less said that it was my fault that he was dead. As if I'm some busybody or something."

Terry started whistling and looked around him as the others laughed. "Ah, poor Abigail, you know we love you."

"Huh, you've got a funny way of showing it."

"What's you being nosy and interfering got to do with his death?"

"I'll ignore that, Terry. But do you remember when we met Carole Newsome that day last year?"

"I do. We couldn't go on our trip to the seaside. She and her husband had been shot, and with our help, Johnson arrested him and his henchman, and he got life. What's that got to do with Trevor?"

"We helped put away Raisin—I mean, Razor Reagan—her ex-husband. And that's how Angie and Johnson got together. If we hadn't got him caught by finding the bodies so quickly, they would never have met."

"If, if, if. Rubbish. Don't worry, love. Upsetting my bird. Couldn't take to that Trevor; as false as my granny's teeth. I didn't like the way he looked at you either."

"Thanks, Terry. I knew you'd understand."

"He'd better not come back here."

"Can we get back to the case?" said Hayley. "Little Lord Bennett could be awake at any minute, and I'd have to go. I know about Martin Reagan and the fact that he's got two brothers, but who is the second suspect?"

"His name is Brydon Hurst. An equally horrible thug who beat a man half to death for saying something to his wife—who then left him. He swore to get Johnson and his family when he got out, and Celia thinks he might have been paroled."

"I'll get Tom to check if he's out and where he is now. Perhaps Jane Nichols or Dave could have a quick look for him. Anything else I should know?"

Abigail said, "Someone's gone to a lot of trouble to frame Johnson. If it wasn't for Trevor seeing a tall man getting rid of the body, even we would have thought it was him."

"We would," said Terry. "He's no saint, but actually, I've never seen him be violent. Rude and obnoxious, yes."

"Don't forget he could have got someone to take the body to the canal for him in his car. But then he'd be open to blackmail for the rest of his life," said Hayley. "And I don't think he's got that many friends."

"What should we do now?" said Betty. "This is usually where you would go and talk to the ex-wife of that Hurst man, Hayley."

"I know. And I definitely won't be going to talk to the two Reagan brothers."

"Do you think they'll charge Johnson?" asked Terry.

"I have no idea. Before they looked in the car, no. And now

they've got means, motive, and the weapon. But if he didn't have the opportunity, he'll be okay. Let's hope he's got an alibi."

Abigail said, "It was Sunday, so chances are he was in the Red Lion till closing time. Tell Tom they should look for a tall man, but Trevor isn't that big himself, so they would look tall to him. And he's met Johnson when they found Angie's body, and he didn't recognise him."

There was a sudden noise from upstairs, and they all looked at each other.

"See what I mean?" said Abigail.

"What, hun?"

"Er, I was telling the others what a lovely, cute little noise Benjamin makes."

"Really? I think it sounds like nothing on earth, and that's after knowing you lot!"

Chapter 35

"Interview commencing at 2 p.m. For the tape, in the room are myself, Chief Inspector Morley, and Sergeant Mills. Interview with Antony Stanley Johnson, who has his solicitor present. Can you confirm your name for the tape, please?"

"You should know it by now, seeing as I'm a superior rank. Detective Chief Inspector Johnson to you."

"Just answer the questions, please, sir. Do you know a woman called Angie Metcalfe?"

"Yes."

"You're aware that her body was found on Monday morning by the canal in Little Frimble?"

"I ought to be. I was the officer in charge when they found her."

"Why didn't you say you knew the victim when you saw the body? You withheld evidence."

"I only saw her briefly, and she had blood on her face. I wasn't sure it was her. I needed to check, so I rang her a couple of times, and she didn't answer. So then I thought it might be her. But I left because it was a double murder, and I wanted to let the Chief Constable know before he saw it on the news. Especially as one of the victims was a famous author. I knew the press would be right on it." Mills was rather impressed with the story. Not a word of truth in it, of course, but quite credible.

"So we can check on your phone that you rang her at that time." Mills thought Morley wasn't quite so daft as he looked. There weren't going to be any phone calls to Angie.

"And what was your relationship with the victim, Angie Metcalfe?"

"I'd been her boyfriend for the last few months. She was the ex of one of the murderers that I put away. She'd already left him years before." His voice broke, and he sniffed. "If you must know, we were planning on getting married later this year. I wouldn't have hurt a hair on her head. Ask Mills."

"Some might think you got her husband convicted so you could live happy families with his wife."

"There was no doubt that the scumbag was guilty. He killed that couple. We found the bodies, and he had the gun, and his DNA was on them. If you ask me, he got one of his mates to kill Angie and frame me."

"We will be checking that. But where were you on Sunday?"

"I went to the Red Lion about midday. Yes, plenty of people saw me, you can check. I got back home at about, er, three. Had something to eat. Then I got a text from Angie at about half four. I was supposed to be going to her flat at seven, but she said she'd come to mine instead."

"Was that unusual?"

"She did come over sometimes, but her flat was much nicer than mine. I was a bit annoyed because it meant I would have to tidy up. I watched a bit of telly and waited for her to come."

"Didn't you worry when she didn't arrive?"

"I didn't know she hadn't. I fell asleep in the chair and didn't wake up till about nine. I tried calling her phone, but she didn't answer, so I left a message. I just assumed something had come up. I thought I'd ring her in the morning." Johnson took a deep breath and was determined not to cry in front of them.

"We haven't found her phone, so we can't confirm your story."

"Story? Check mine then. Her phone was always in her bag. Haven't you found it?"

"No, we haven't, sir. Did you see anyone when you were at home?"

"Just the butler. 'Course I didn't."

Mills asked, "Was it usual for you to sleep for that long in the day? No offence, it's not like you aren't used to having a few too many."

"It was, Dave. I haven't slept that long for ages. I don't even sleep that long when I'm in bed. Do you think I was drugged? That would explain a lot."

Mills asked, "What did you eat and drink when you got back?"

"I had a pie out of the fridge and a bag of crisps. And a couple of whiskies. You need to check that bottle. Someone must have put something in it."

"How would they have got into your flat? Don't tell me, you keep a key under the mat," said Morley.

Johnson suddenly remembered something. "No, but I left a spare set of keys at Angie's. I just thought. That's how. I got a taxi home one night. I'd had a skinful, and when I went the next day to pick my car up, I'd left my keys at home. So from then on, I left a spare set there."

"Did we find a spare set of keys, Mills? No, I didn't think so. So, we've only got your word for it. I think you're spinning us a yarn, Tony. You're telling us that someone killed Mrs Metcalfe after you got back from the pub, picked up your car after drugging you, went to her flat, drove to the canal, dumped her body, killed Trevor Grand, and put your car back with the bottle, bag, and shoe inside."

"Yes, thank you."

"I was being sarcastic, sir. Not likely, is it? More likely that you got to your girlfriend's house, argued, you killed her, wiped off your fingerprints and put her in your boot once it had got dark. You drove to Carlton Bridge to dump the body. Unfortunately for you, Trevor Grand was on his way back from the pub. You hit him, followed him back to the boat, and killed him. I'm thinking Angie Metcalfe told you it was over. She was well out of your league. Maybe she'd had enough of roughing it."

That did it for Johnson. He leapt over the table and tried to grab Morley by the throat. Mills pulled him off and got him to get back on his chair.

"Well, for the tape, I think we can see that DCI Johnson has got a temper. We found your prints on the murder weapon—a heavy glass bottle. Seems she was hit just once with it. How did they manage to get your prints on that?"

"I admit we shared a bottle of bubbly last week. I opened it. I bought it for when we were arranging the wedding. So finding my prints on that bottle doesn't prove a thing. He must have worn gloves. And why would I have been so stupid as to leave her bag and the murder weapon in my car?"

"I can think of a lot of reasons. You didn't have time, you forgot. Or more likely, if you had the chance, you were going to frame someone else. You didn't realise how quick we'd be on to you. If you're charged, we'll be checking your flat for anything with blood on, like your coat and shoes."

"Search all you like. I've got nothing to hide." Maybe a few stolen cigarettes and an envelope of money from one of his friends that he turned a blind eye to, but no blood, he thought.

"Interview suspended at 2.19 pm. Could I see you outside for a moment, please, Sergeant?"

They went into the corridor and asked PC Coult to wait in the interview room.

Mills was not happy. "You were deliberately provoking him."

"Just showing him in his true colours. And it's sir."

"It could have happened how he said, sir. I've worked with him for over four years, and he's never been violent before. Mouthy and a bigot, yes. But I find it hard to believe he would kill two people in cold blood. Actually, since he'd been with Angie, he'd turned into a much nicer person."

"So he got a heart, and then she smashed it to pieces. That's how I see it," said Morley. He was already eyeing up his promotion once he'd got rid of the DCI. He might keep Mills if he stopped disagreeing with him.

"We've got to let him go tomorrow if we don't find more evidence, sir."

"So go and find me some then, Mills."

Mills agreed, but he wanted to find the evidence that showed his boss was innocent. After he went back to his desk, he read a text from Tom and called him back to tell him about the interview and what he was going to do. He was the only other one in the station who thought the boss wasn't guilty. Tom said that the person they were looking for was tall, taller than Johnson. He didn't ask how he knew. And also that a thug called Brydon Hurst had threatened Johnson as he was being led from the court, and he could be out now. So he sat at his desk, entered Hurst's name and found out that he had been released five weeks ago after being found guilty of GBH and was released for good behaviour. Mills rang his probation officer and found out that his address was near the village of Boxford.

The next check he made was on any associates of Martin Reagan. He found he had two brothers who also lived in Gorebridge. He'd call on them later with a few constables, but for now, he went and asked PC Jane Nichols to go with him to check Johnson's house to find the whisky and anything else that could have sleeping pills in it. After that, he decided he would have another search of Angie's flat for her phone. If someone had texted Johnson, he might have taken his gloves off to use it.

Often, a little slip-up like that could be enough to catch someone. On an impulse, he sent a copy of the interview to Tom. He knew he could lose his job, but he didn't trust Morley. At least Johnson was fair; he was equally horrible to everyone. He picked up the keys to both flats, and Mills and Jane left together.

Chapter 36

ABIGAIL COULDN'T TAKE THE NOT KNOWING ANY longer, so she decided to just pop over to Hayley's on the off chance. She would pretend it was to see how the baby was. Of course, if there happened to be any news on Johnson, that would be good.

Tom wasn't there, but Hayley was, changing a particularly gross nappy in the sitting room when she arrived.

"For the first time, I'm glad I can't smell anymore, Hayley."

"I bet you are. Far more comes out of him than goes in, that's for sure."

"How did you sleep last night?"

"He can sleep for three hours at a time now, so that's better. But I don't care, hun. I love him so much. I just hold him in bed with me and stare at his little face. I can't believe he's mine."

"He is gorgeous. How is Tom?"

"That's the first time you've ever asked that. Do you mean has Tom got any news? If I didn't know better, I would think that was why you came," Hayley said, smiling. She knew her too well.

"Oh, okay, yes. Has Tom got any more news?"

"The interview with Inspector Morley didn't go too well. He was all over Tony. Even goaded him into throwing a punch. Do you want to hear it? Mills made a copy and sent it over in case we had any ideas. I think Tony might have asked him to. Morley would go mad. I think he's after the DCI job if he can get him convicted. Do you want to listen to it?"

"Er, does Benjie cry?" Abigail joked. It was the first time that she had ever listened to an interview, and she was fascinated. It made her wish even more that she had gone into the police force while she could. Although she would have wanted to go straight in as a detective.

"So what is Mills doing next?"

"You heard Johnson thinks he may have been drugged, so he's going to his flat to take some samples. He hadn't realised she hadn't arrived because he'd passed out."

"I'm thinking that isn't too unusual for him on a Sunday afternoon. Anything else?"

"After Johnson's flat, he's going to Angie's to have another look around before he goes and questions Hurst. He's getting the names of the Reagan brothers as well."

"I haven't been to where Angie was murdered. I went to see Celia while the others went. I might get Terry to go with me. There might be some clues they've missed. If only we could get there in time to catch Mills while he's still there."

"If you're dropping a hint that you want a lift, you're going to be disappointed, hun."

"Me? As if I would do that!"

"I don't feel up to driving yet. And not only that, apparently you have to be an engineer to get the baby seat in."

"Don't worry, Terry loves getting the bus. He'll probably think it's romantic or something. Then we can get a lift by Sergeant Mills to see Hurst. He'll never know."

"I feel so surplus to requirements. You won't need me soon."

"You're joking, we all miss you like crazy. It's doubled the work. I needn't have gone to Gorebridge today, and you could have just asked Tom what happened. And I miss my best friend."

"That's so sweet. When Tom's gone back to work, I'll be able to go out. We've got the pushchair ready. I think he's got to be a few weeks older yet. But I have a feeling he'll love going to the library. At least I'll have an excuse for going so often. Benjie will be having a lot of bedtime stories."

Hayley shushed Abigail and turned up the television.

A woman was reading the news. "And now back to the Canal Murders. We've just learned that a man has been arrested on suspicion of the murders of Angie Metcalfe and the writer, Trevor Grand. We have no other details other than that he is from Gorebridge."

"Poor Johnson," said Hayley. "You'd better get going. I have a feeling you and the agency are the only ones that can save him."

With the bags of evidence from Johnson's flat in his boot, Mills parked outside Angie's flat. His first job tomorrow was getting the whisky tested for drugs. If Johnson received a text at half past four, at least they had a rough time of death. So Jane knocked at the two downstairs flats and asked them if they had seen anything at about that time on the day of the murder.

Terry and Abigail arrived as Mills was walking up the stairs of Banbury Court. When the three of them reached the top, Hilda Waterman flew out of her door.

"I thought it was you, Sergeant. Is there any news of our neighbour and that poor man on his boat? I heard you arrested someone. Is it the man I told you about? What if it's not him and he comes back?"

"I think you're safe, Mrs Waterman."

"Well, why have you come back?"

"And you think I'm nosy, Terry," said Abigail.

Mills said, "We're still following our enquiries. Is your neighbour home?"

"If he's up. He worked last night and got back at about eight o'clock this morning."

"Thank you, Mrs Waterman," and he waited until she reluctantly shut her door. He wished she had been home on the day of the murder. Then he knocked at number seven.

Sean White opened his door a few inches. "Oh, it's you. There's nothing more I can tell you."

"Can I come in? It won't take long." Mills could have talked at the door, but he couldn't be sure that the nosy neighbour wouldn't be listening through her letterbox.

They stood in his hall. "We know that a text was sent from Mrs Metcalfe's phone between four and five. Did you hear anything or see anyone arrive?"

"I told you, no. I had the telly on, and I can't see the road from my windows. Ask Nosy Rosy. Nothing goes on that she doesn't know about."

"Mrs Waterman and her husband go to their daughter's on a Sunday."

"Bet she hated that, all that happening when she wasn't here. She had no time for Angie. Jealous, you see. She couldn't hold a candle to her."

"Thank you, Mr White. Let me know if you think of anything else."

Terry interrupted, "The nosy neighbour said he had a soft spot for Angie. He hasn't got an alibi. And he was in his flat on his own."

"We can't rule him out. Unrequited love is as powerful a motive as a million pounds, Terry. He's the right build as well."

Sergeant Mills lifted the yellow tape across the door of flat eight and went inside as Jane joined him.

"No one can remember anything else at that time, sir. Nobody saw any cars or people that shouldn't be here."

"Let's hope we find the victim's phone. Look everywhere, Jane. Oh, and see if you can find Johnson's spare set of keys. He reckons he kept them here because he left them at his house once after he'd got a taxi back." But they soon realised neither his keys nor Angie's phone were there.

"Do you think the phone was thrown in the canal, sir?"

"Probably, Jane. But I don't think the CC will go to the expense of having it dredged. I was thinking, if they went to all the trouble of framing Johnson, why would they get rid of it with his name and number? If the neighbour hadn't seen his car, and he'd remembered to take his toothbrush and glass, we might never have known."

Abigail had to agree. "That's a very good point. Opens up a lot more possibilities."

"Not to me," admitted Terry. "Looks like they're going. Shall we go with them?"

"Definitely. He's going to see Brydon Hurst now. The one that threatened Johnson. I hope it's our side of Becklesfield."

"We could get the bus back."

"Buses are so slow. Do they have to stop so many times?" moaned Abigail.

"Er, yes, so people can get on and off."

"But it's always when I'm in a hurry."

"You're always in a hurry, Abigail. Especially if there's been a murder."

"I miss Hayley," sighed Abigail. "And not just for the lifts she gives us. I'll have to tell you how we came to be friends one day."

"I thought she was a sewing customer."

"She was, but that wasn't how we met. That was the strangest thing you've ever heard. One night in the library, when we've got no cases, I'll tell you all about it."

"I look forward to that, but let's get in Dave's car quick," said Terry.

And Abigail was lucky because Mills told Jane that they were going to question an ex-con called Hurst, and it was only two miles from Becklesfield.

Fifteen minutes later, they were outside a sixties terraced house on a council estate. A small child opened the door.

"Is your daddy home?" Jane asked.

"DAD!"

A short, broad-shouldered man went to see who was there. "Can I help you?"

"Are you Brydon Hurst, sir? We're from Gorebridge Police."

"What's he done now? You'd better come in. Feel free to cart him off. He's the wife's brother, so he's staying here till he sorts himself out or goes back inside. She's at work. Go in the kitchen, I'll go and get him. We've had to put the kids in one bedroom, so he spends most of the time up there. Brydon! Cops! I'll keep the kids in with me."

A tall, thickset man with greasy hair joined them in the kitchen, and Mills regretted bringing Jane rather than a couple of the other constables.

"Brydon Hurst? I'm Sergeant Mills, and this is WPC Nichols. We're investigating two murders and would like to know your whereabouts for the Sunday before last."

"Murder? I never killed anyone in my life. And you can't prove I did. Who am I supposed to have killed?"

"Just answer the question, please, sir."

"I was here. I'm always here. No money to go anywhere else. You can ask them. Can't get a job thanks to you lot. Why do you think I killed someone?"

"At your trial, you threatened Detective Chief Inspector Johnson."

Hurst smiled broadly. "Brilliant, someone got him, did they? Couldn't have happened to a nicer copper. Hope it was nothing too quick."

"DCI Johnson is not dead."

"Well, what are you on about then? You don't mean those canal murders, do you? That was a Sunday. I didn't even know the pair of them. Ask me sister, she'll tell you. I was nowhere near there."

Abigail believed him. And so did Mills.

Chapter 37

THE FOLLOWING MORNING WAS FRIDAY, NEARLY TWO weeks since Angie and Trevor were brutally murdered. Friday was always an exciting day for the ghosts in the library, as the Chiltern Weekly was delivered good and early.

The article they hadn't wanted to read was on the front page.

Man Charged with the Canal Murders

A 55-year-old man was charged yesterday with the murders of Angie Metcalfe and author Trevor Grand. Their bodies were found at Little Frimble.

The man is thought to be Antony Stanley Johnson of Gorebridge. He has been granted bail and will appear before magistrates on 30th May at Gorebridge Crown Court.

Betty was relieved. "At least he got bail. Imagine if he was kept in custody, he wouldn't have lasted a day. Is there any hope for him, Abigail? I know he is a most unpleasant man, but I feel rather sorry for him."

"I think he's had it," said Terry.

Lillian agreed. "Although Tom told Mills the man was taller than Johnson, with no witnesses, Inspector Morley isn't going to take any notice. He sounds awful. Makes Johnson seem nice. I reckon he's after his job."

"Come on, Abigail," said Suzie. "You usually know who it is by now."

"I'm really trying. There's a few things that I've heard in the last couple of days that don't add up. But I never was very good at sums. Someone said something that wasn't quite right. It's gone now."

Betty said, "So let's go through all the facts, like Hayley always does. Go on, Abigail, you go first."

"Okay. Tom told Hayley that they had looked into Angie, and she didn't seem to have any enemies. Nothing was stolen from her flat, so not a robbery. So it must have something to do with Johnson. We overheard Mills saying he was going to see Reagan's brothers, but with some larger constables than Jane. So it could be both or one of them. There's the very nasty Brydon Hurst. Mills has to check his alibi, but I don't think his brother-in-law would cover for him. The sister might, though."

"I bet there's a lot of old prisoners it could be," said Terry. "We can't know them all. Don't forget that neighbour, Sean White. He was in love with Angie, I could tell."

Betty said, "You know what they say about unregurgitated love."

"She was a beautiful woman for her age. I'm sure a lot fancied her," added Lillian.

Abigail sighed. "Yes, beautiful people can cause a lot of jealousy. I should know," she said modestly, looking at Terry. "But why not kill Johnson? It would have been a lot easier for the neighbour to bash him on the head and get rid of any competition. No, this was personal. They wanted to ruin him professionally and emotionally as well. Is there anyone who would benefit from putting him in jail?"

"The whole police station would be happier, for a start," said Lillian.

"That's it, Lillian. I've got it." The others all looked at Abigail and frowned. "Inspector Morley would get his job! Mills said he'd been there years without a promotion. If he caught the Canal Murders and put Johnson away, he'd be the CC's favourite. I remember what I heard now. In the interview, he said Johnson must have been seen by Trevor when he was getting rid of the body, and he hit him and then followed him to the boat. Ta-da. How would he have known that? The doctor didn't even know—you told us that, Lillian. She thought he was hit seconds before he was stabbed."

Suzie clapped. "I knew you'd do it, Abigail. You're the best."

"Not exactly a smoking gun, is it?" said Terry. "He could have just guessed."

"I believe you, Abigail."

"Thank you, Suzie. Although, there's still something not right. I've missed something. So Morley is a probable but not a definite."

Betty counted a list on her fingers. "So we've got the Reagan brothers, or anyone that Raisin Reagan sent to do the job. Brydon Hurst, Inspector Morley, or some unknown stalker of Angie."

Terry said, "Don't forget the neighbour, White. He was tall. Or, I hate to say it, Johnson might have done it." Terry laughed. "He might have had heels on."

Abigail leaned back, closed her eyes, and began moving the clues about in her mind. She was mumbling this time. "He said that, then she said that. But no, that can't have happened. Unless, what did they say? But then ..." All was quiet again.

"She's nodded off," said Terry.

"Well, she can't be dead," said Lillian.

"I'm thinking," Abigail said at last. "Hmm. It could be."

"You know who the murderer is?" said Betty. "Do tell us, dear. So you were right—it's Inspector Morley?"

"Er, no. I don't think it is now. Listen to what I tell you and then let me know what you think."

"How come you always have to be in charge?" asked Lillian. She didn't think Abigail had any idea who the murderer was.

"You know what they say, Lillian—cream rises to the top," Abigail told her.

"So does algae," mumbled Lillian. "Go on, then."

Abigail ignored Lillian's comments. They often clashed, and it was like water off a duck's back to Abigail. So she got to her feet and stood against one of the bookcases, more to annoy Lillian than anything else. The others stifled a giggle, as they knew she liked to stand by a fireplace as if she was Poirot.

She put her hands behind her back and began. "From the beginning, this was a very singular case. That had you. I know you think I want to be Hercule Poirot, but I fancy a bit of Sherlock today. In fact, a three-pipe problem, if we are allowed to say that these days. Yes, it was a very singular case—the murder of Inspector Lestrade's beau, I mean Inspector Johnson's beau. She was the woman. His Irene Adler. Elementary, you might say."

Betty interrupted Abigail. "What was it Holmes used to say? 'When you have the impossible, but the truth is eliminated'. Or 'however eliminated is the improbable, it's impossible, so must be the truth'."

"Thank you, Watson. I think I'd better forget about Sherlock. Where was I? But I will take your advice, Betty, and try to eliminate—not the truth, but some of the victims. Then what's left is possible and could well be the truth. Oh God, you've got me at it now. I'd better start again.

I think we can eliminate either one of the Reagan brothers; they're hardened criminals and much too savvy to get rid of a body on the only bit of canal round there that has two barges moored with people living on them. And it's close to Carlton Bridge, where someone could have seen them or a car. Yes, they wanted the body to be found, but not to be seen themselves. And I think they would have taken their own weapon.

If it was Inspector Morley, he wouldn't have got rid of Angie's phone. We all know what Johnson's like. There would have been bound to be something on there that could incriminate him in other things. And did he know that Johnson was seeing someone? We have to check, but how did he know Johnson had a girlfriend? I think he worked out of another CID.

From what I saw of Brydon Hurst, I don't think it's him. He's wallowing in self-pity about not getting a job or having enough money. And I think if he came home at night covered in blood, his sister would have noticed. Having two small children in the house, she wouldn't risk them.

So that just leaves the neighbour. When Jane asked at the other flats if they had seen a car there on the Sunday afternoon, they said none that shouldn't be there."

"Didn't I say it was Sean White?" said Terry.

Abigail ignored him. "The biggest clues are the phone, the interview, and the fact that Trevor was killed on his boat. Now, who would bother to get rid of the phone? Not the Reagans—they wanted her death to point to her latest boyfriend. They didn't know the neighbour would know it was Johnson. Same with anyone else trying to frame him. No, I think he was framed not because he was a policeman, but because he was Angie's boyfriend. She was the target, not him.

I think the murderer killed her in a rage, hence the blood spatter and force. It wasn't planned. But a look on her phone showed that Johnson was due there, so he was told not to come and that Angie would go over there instead. It was so unfair, but she was killed because she attracted men. Nothing that she had done."

"So Terry was right, it was the neighbour," said Betty.

"He was right. Just not the neighbour he thought."

"What? It was that quiet, henpecked man, Howard?" said Lillian in disbelief.

"No. I'm pretty sure the one that killed her was his wife, Hilda!"

Chapter 38

"Hold your horses, Abigail," said Terry. "You've lost me. We know it was a man that did it."

"We only know it was a man that got rid of the body and stabbed Trevor. And who better to bully into doing that than her poor husband?"

"But that's a bit of a stretch—getting Johnson's car, putting the body in, and setting him up."

"It was quite easy, actually. They couldn't do much until it was dark. I'm guessing they came across a set of keys for a Toyota and went from there. They put the body in their own car and then over to Johnson's. Hilda had heard him give his address to the taxi driver. Jane said the neighbours below said the only cars there were the ones that are usually there. I expect there's a blanket or a rug they used to move Angie. Then they drove back from the canal, picked up their car, left Johnson's outside his flat, and went home. And they could have got rid of their bloody clothes anywhere."

"What about the phone and the interview you were saying was a clue?" asked Suzie. "And what was the motive? Jealousy?"

"A bit more than that. We won't know how friendly Howard

was with Angie until we look at Howard's phone. But I think in the past they might have been more than friends, and Hilda would think there might be calls or texts between Angie and her husband. Although, I think it was more on his side and he wouldn't leave her alone. Something must have happened on that Sunday. Didn't Hilda say they took parcels in for her? Perhaps he was dropping one off and stayed that bit too long. When Mills talked to them that first day, you said Howard stuck up for her when Hilda said she was a brassy blonde, and he said she wasn't. He knew because he'd seen a photo of her when she was young. I saw that—it was the only one there, and it was in her bedroom."

"But they were at their daughter's house, dear."

"Terry said her exact words were, 'We usually go to our daughter's on a Sunday.' Not quite the same, is it? But Mills will be able to check."

Suzie excitedly asked, "So what was it that made you even think of her?"

"When I saw the paper today and remembered what she had said yesterday."

Suzie looked at the Chiltern Weekly again. "I don't see it—Man Charged with the Canal Murders."

"Exactly. Whenever it's been on the news or in the paper, it's been referred to as the Canal Murders, but Hilda Waterman asked about Angie's murder when I was there. And about the poor man on his boat! How did she know where he was killed?"

"She's right," said Terry. "I heard it myself. The police wouldn't have given out that sort of information. You can go to the top of the class, Abi. And just for that, I'll take you out on a date tomorrow night."

"Well, thank you, kind sir. But what can we do now? Johnson's been charged."

"Um, well, we can't do this without Hayley, can we?" said Lillian. "Once they've got their names as suspects, the police can check with their daughter for their alibi and find anything with blood on it in the flat."

"I would say there's no rush, but they might burn the clothes and even get rid of the car. That will have evidence in it. Even if it's just one drop of blood," said Abigail.

"And I think the husband will fold like a cheap suit once the police find out it was them. He was only covering up for her. I wonder if he was there as she killed the poor lady. I'd love to be a fly on the wall at her interview," said Terry.

Terry and Abigail weren't so much flies on the wall as ghosts in the corner at the interview of Hilda Millicent Waterman. Hayley had passed on all the information to Dave Mills, and he didn't ask how she knew. He didn't want to know. Mills was just glad he hadn't questioned the Reagan gang yet. Morley still didn't know how Mills had worked it out. He'd had all the information, and it had never occurred to him to check the neighbour's alibi. And to top it all off, Johnson had been exonerated and given two weeks' compassionate leave. So he was in no mood to question this woman who was the cause of all his troubles.

"Hilda Millicent Waterman, you've been arrested for the murders of Angie Metcalfe and Trevor Grand."

"Absolute rubbish, Inspector. I had nothing to do with it. My husband killed her and the author."

"That's funny because he's saying you killed your neighbour, and he only helped you to hide the fact. He told us in his interview that you've always been jealous of her and were convinced that they were having a relationship."

"And he said he hadn't, huh. And you believed him? I thought it had finished once she met that funny little man."

"Do you mean Detective Chief Inspector Antony Johnson?"

"Well, I didn't know he was a policeman. He didn't look like one to me."

"So, what happened on the day of the murders, Mrs Waterman? You lied and told my sergeant that you were at your daughter's."

"No, I said we usually went to our daughter's. We didn't go that day. I didn't lie, and it's not my fault if he misunderstood me." She gave a faint smile. "My daughter said her children had a stomach bug, so not to come. Later on, I wondered where Howard was; he was nowhere in the flat. Then I noticed the package that came for her the day before had gone. But after about fifteen minutes, I went to check. The door was on the latch, and I went in, trying to listen to see what they were up to. I went into the kitchen, and he was just lifting up an empty bottle and bringing it down on her head. I was horrified, Inspector."

"You see, that's where your husband tells the story a bit differently. He said he'd given her the package, and Angie was just making him a coffee to say thank you. They were laughing and having fun—something he never gets with you, I should think. And you saw red. You picked up the bottle and hit her from behind."

"Well, he would say that, wouldn't he? I think I heard her saying that he was too old and he was only good for doing jobs around the place."

"He says he loved her and would never hurt her," said Morley. "If he was going to hit anyone over the head with a bottle, I'm guessing it would be you."

"We've been married for thirty years, Inspector," said Hilda.

"Exactly. I'm more inclined to believe him, and I think the jury will."

"But it's my word against his, isn't it?"

"Not necessarily, but we'll come back to that. So, you both have a dead body. What do you do then?"

"Howard begged me to help him—he always was useless in a crisis. I took charge then. He's my husband; I can't see the jury punishing me for wanting to help my husband. I went to our flat and got an old duvet cover to wrap her in. We were going to take her in her own car and park it somewhere, but then I saw the keys for the Toyota and thought it would be much better to put the blame on her latest fling."

"And get me in trouble, thanks. How did you know where his car was? It wasn't outside."

"I'd heard him tell the taxi driver one night. I didn't know the number of the flat, but it was parked in the car park. It was easy enough to find. So we parked next to it and transferred the body to his boot."

"Who drove to Little Frimble?"

"I did. Howard is a useless driver. I parked on the bridge, and he lifted out the body. He had one job. One job. And he couldn't even do that properly. He let someone see him. It was dark, and he needn't have killed the man. But no, he hit him and then followed him till he was on his barge and stabbed him with something. He blamed me for that. He said I would have made his life a misery if he'd left a witness."

"You probably would, to be fair. Poor guy," Morley said sadly. "That was the first clue. You slipped up, Mrs Waterman, not your husband. You knew Trevor Grand had been killed on his boat. That fact was never released."

"Well, I'm not admitting to killing anyone. And you can't prove I have."

"Funnily enough, we can—and we have you to thank for that."

For the first time, Hilda looked worried. "What do you mean?"

"We've searched your flat. Seems you disposed of the clothes that you were wearing but kept your husband's. Very good of you. We found them in a black bag in a suitcase in your spare room. No doubt so you could use his bloody clothes as leverage and make his life even more of a misery than you already did."

"It just proves he's guilty and no proof I was involved."

"Have you heard of forensics and something called blood spatter?"

"Of course. I watch TV."

"His coat has traces of smeared blood from Mrs Metcalfe, and spots of blood from when he stabbed Mr Grand. But underneath, on his shirt, he has blood spatter from the kitchen?"

"Well, there you go then," Hilda said haughtily.

"Not quite. There's only blood on the left side of his clothes, consistent with what he says—that you killed her and were standing in front of him. Your husband is right-handed; the blood would have been all over the right side of his shirt and trousers. He's a tall man. We checked, and there's a Hilda-sized shape in front of him."

"I'm not admitting anything. Whatever happened, it was him. I shall plead not guilty. It was his fault. If he'd left her alone, it would never have happened, and he'd be at home with me. I hope he rots in jail."

"I have a feeling you both will, Mrs Waterman," Morley said as he collected up his paperwork and told Sergeant Mills to formally charge her.

Terry looked at Abigail. "I don't know about you, but I think if I was married to her, I'd rather be in jail!"

Chapter 39

SUMMER HAD ARRIVED, AND HAYLEY WAS BEGINNING to feel more like her old self. Benjie was letting her get six hours most nights—something she would have said was a bad night not long ago. And gone was any chance of a lie-in. At least Luna was happy about that. He liked to get up early and snooze all day himself.

With difficulty, Hayley managed to get the pushchair through the library door. She was excited to catch up with all the others, but she couldn't get to the back. Every few steps, she was stopped by the villagers, who wanted to see the new addition to their numbers.

In the end, she gave up and took out three picture books for Benjie. As Hayley checked them out, the only question Janine wanted to know was how Luna was getting on with the baby. Hayley had given her a kitten, and they always chatted about their furry babies.

"He was very unsure at first. Well, actually, he was sure he didn't like the baby at all. But on the second day, Luna got a bit closer and tapped him very gently with his paw. It was so sweet,

I nearly cried. Then he snuggled up very gently, and they rubbed heads. I'm not sure it was that hygienic, but what can you do? Now they're like best friends. Trouble is, Benjie can go from sound asleep to a foghorn faster than the speed of light, so Luna's off like a hat in a hurricane. It is funny. I need to get some videos of them together."

"So he's not jealous of you holding the baby then?"

"I wouldn't say that. But if cats are capable of giving dirty looks, Tom definitely gets them when he's holding Benjie. He's always been Luna's favourite, even though it's me that looks after him."

"It's nice they'll grow up together," said Janette. "But how are you, Hayley?"

"Tired but happy. Actually, I can rest more now that Tom's back at work. And Benjie sleeps better, so that's amazing. I just look forward to the day when he'll sleep for at least nine hours."

"I think it'll be a while yet. Maybe fifteen years."

"Oh, don't say that, Janette. Right, it's such a nice day today, I think I'll have a walk round the park and sit by the swings," said Hayley, loud enough for the waiting ghosts to hear.

Abigail, Terry and Betty followed her out, trying to get a glimpse of the baby, who was still fast asleep and wrapped up tight. They walked past the florist shop and were very pleased to see Mrs Merry serving customers again.

"Can't you get him out, Hayley? I want to see my little godson," said Abigail.

"Are you mad?" said Hayley. "As much as I love him, it's lovely when he's asleep."

"Any news on Howard and Hilda Waterman?" asked Terry.

"Tom found out their court case will be in September. They won't get out before then. She's going to plead not guilty, but he's pleading guilty and hoping for a lesser sentence. His lawyers say that he'll only plead guilty if he's not sent to the same prison as Reagan. But I have a feeling that he'll be able to get to both of them. Tom reckons within a year both of them will have been accidentally stabbed while taking a shower. Hilda Waterman is still saying her husband did it all, but I don't think the jury will agree."

"Good. Horrible woman," said Betty.

"I know what I was going to ask you," said Hayley. "Where did Trevor Grand go? Did he pass over?"

"He passed on Abigail, and went over to Celia, by all accounts," said Terry. "His loss, darling."

"Good. After the way he treated me, I wouldn't want him here. And he spends most of his time at his ex-wife's house. To see the children, supposedly. Anyway, that's enough about him. Is Johnson back at work yet?" asked Abigail.

"Tomorrow, apparently."

"Did he ever thank you for helping him?"

"Nothing yet. He's had a few weeks off, so you never know."

A grizzle came from the pushchair.

"Oh good, he's awake," said Abigail. "Hello, little Benjie, I'm your fairy godmother. Hayley, he smiled at me!"

"It's wind," said Terry.

"I'm telling you, he smiled," she insisted.

"He hasn't even smiled at me and Tom yet. Let me get him out, and we'll both try."

But Abigail was right. Benjamin had saved his first smiles for her, proving to everyone that not only was he psychic, but, as Abigail said, he had very good taste.

Before Benjamin could start waking the dead—those that weren't already awake—Hayley went back to her house in Church Lane. As she got closer, she could see a dark blue Toyota. DCI Johnson got out and followed her to the front door.

"Hello, Tony, you'll have to come in; someone's hungry."

"Just for a minute then. She's a beautiful lass."

"Yes, he is."

"Oh yeah, sorry."

"Do you want a cup of tea?"

"No, I'm not stopping. I've told Tom, and I want you to know …"

"It's fine, you don't have to thank me."

Tony looked surprised. "I wasn't going to. I got a bit carried away when I asked for your help. I don't know what I was thinking. Must have been the grief. And in the end, the truth came out with good old-fashioned police work. I trained Sergeant Mills well, as it happens. I told him it's more important to look for the lies than the truth. He was the one who noticed that the Waterman woman slipped up and said Grand was murdered on his barge, and his enquiries got him there in the end. It was more Morley that stitched me up. I don't believe in all your hocus pocus. No offence."

"I do find it slightly offensive, if I'm honest."

"Well, I daresay you get some schmucks who want your services. But not me. And I told Tom he won't get any special treatment from me from now on. We're back to where we were; I'm his superior officer, and he's still my police constable. So I don't want to hear you getting involved in my cases again. I wanted to get that straight."

"Oh, it's as straight as a witch's broom, Inspector, believe me."

"I'd better look out—you'll be putting a curse on me," he joked as he walked to the door, whereupon he tripped up on the corner of the mat.

"Yes, you'd better watch your step," Hayley told him as her eyes narrowed menacingly. "It is a shame, though."

"What's a shame?" said Johnson, looking a bit worried.

"I know Sergeant Mills is good, but he doesn't have what I have."

"Oh yes? And what's that? A cauldron?"

"Very funny. No, a message from Angie."

That stopped Johnson in his tracks.

"What message? How did you get a message?"

"I think you'd call it hocus pocus. She said how sorry she is that you won't be able to get married. And she thanks you for the best day of her life when you went away together. It was at the Claythorne Hotel …"

"Claybourne," said Johnson, while his heart thumped. "What else?"

"She said she was sorry that she beat you at the mini-golf. And how funny it was when that huge seagull made you scream like a girl when he tried to take a chip."

Johnson gave a faint smile and asked, "Anything else?"

Hayley would have loved to have said, 'And make sure you're nice to everyone', but she just said, "Only that she really loved you, and to have a good life, and she hopes you meet someone else. Then she went. It was last night. I don't think she'll be back."

"Well, thank you for that, Hayley."

He was looking down, but then he suddenly lifted his head and became the old Johnson again.

"Not that I believe a word of it. And this doesn't change anything. I'm still Detective Chief Inspector Johnson, and you're still my constable's daft hippy wife. Right, I'll be off then."

His phone rang, and he answered it.

"What is it, Mills? Right, right. I'll take it. See you there. No rest for the wicked, Hayley. There's been a murder. Got to go—people to see, murderers to catch."

He went off without a look back at Hayley, who took Benjamin out of his pushchair and put him in his Moses basket.

"Let's see if Nanny Bennett wants to come and babysit her darling grandson, shall we, poppet? There's no way I'm going to let that awful man solve that murder. It's time The Deadly Detective Agency was back open for business."

The End

Acknowledgments

A special thank you to Miika Hannila at Next Chapter Publishing.
And to Petteri Hannila for the excellent layout.
Also, many thanks to Lordan June Pinote, who has done another excellent cover.

About the Author

Ann Parker was born in Hertfordshire, England, and still lives there with her husband, Terry, and her black and white cat, Jazz.

She is the author of the bestselling Abigail Summers Cozy Mysteries—The Deadly Detective Agency, The Deadly Pub Quiz, The Deadly Regatta, The Deadly Fun Run, and The Deadly Wedding.

Her children's short stories and poems are available in the book entitled Magic & Memories.

Ann has had her poems published on Spillwords and in the bestselling anthologies, Hidden in Childhood and Petals of Haiku, as well as various magazines.

When she is not writing, she loves spending time with her family, watching cricket, or reading a good whodunit.

To learn more about Ann Parker and discover more Next Chapter authors, visit our website at www.nextchapter.pub.

Printed in Dunstable, United Kingdom

67160139R00139